SAMUEL BECKETT

Waiting for Godot

Preface by Mary Bryden

faber and faber

Originally published as *En attendant Godot* by
Les Éditions de Minuit, Paris, 1952

First published in the United States in 1974 in the author's translation by
Grove Press. First published in Great Britain by Faber and Faber in 1956.
Corrected text published by Faber and Faber in 1965

This edition first published in 2010
by Faber and Faber Ltd
Bloomsbury House
74–77 Great Russell Street
London WC1B 3DA

Typeset by RefineCatch Limited, Bungay, Suffolk
Printed in England by CPI Group (UK) Ltd, Croydon, CRO 4YY

All applications for performing rights should be addressed to
Curtis Brown Ltd, 4th Floor, Haymarket House, 28/29 Haymarket,
London SW1 4ST

The right of Samuel Beckett to be identified as author of this work
has been asserted in accordance with Section 77 of the Copyright,
Designs and Patents Act 1988

The right of Mary Bryden to be identified as editor of this work
has been asserted in accordance with Section 77 of the Copyright,
Designs and Patents Act 1988

A CIP record for this book
is available from the British Library

ISBN 978–0–571–24459–1

Contents

Preface

Literary futures are sometimes unpredictable. Honoré de Balzac, unsatisfied with fame as a novelist, dreamt fruitlessly of becoming a great playwright. Samuel Beckett once confided that he considered his sequence or 'trilogy' of post-war novels to be his most important work. Yet slipped in between the composition of the second and third volumes (*Malone meurt* and *L'Innommable*) was a two-act play that he claimed to have written 'as relaxation, to get away from the awful prose I was writing at that time'.[1] Such was *En attendant Godot*, later to be acclaimed by many as the greatest play of the twentieth century.

On the day Beckett began composing the play – Saturday, 9 October 1948 – the London theatre scene hardly seemed to be waiting for *Godot*. That evening, theatregoers had a range of options which included the usual variety of farces and musicals, an American ice show, plays by established writers such as Terence Rattigan and George Bernard Shaw, a production of *Doctor Faustus* at the Old Vic, and one or two new offerings, such as Tennessee Williams's *The Glass Menagerie* at the Haymarket Theatre. Yet, within a few years, *Godot* was to force a reconsideration of what theatre was and what it could be. In 1955, the critic Kenneth Tynan would remark that the play had prompted him to reflect on the rules governing drama, 'and, having done so, to pronounce them not elastic enough. It is validly new.'[2]

The journey through text, transmission and reception was, however, a long and complex one. In 1948, Beckett had recently emerged from the uncertainties and traumas of the Occupation in France, much of which he had spent in hiding, with his partner Suzanne, in the unoccupied southern zone. Even if cultural life in capitals like London and Paris might appear to be enjoying a renewed vibrancy, daily life in large parts of Europe was still overshadowed by shortages and by political, economic and social instabilities. Indeed, on that October weekend in 1948 when Beckett began to write *Godot*, northern France was in turmoil as a result of a miners' strike; police used tear gas in Nancy to break up crowds of demonstrators; railwaymen were planning to strike in support of the miners; and merchant seamen had already halted cross-Channel steamers between Dieppe and Newhaven. Only half of the northern power stations were running, and the threat of electricity rationing loomed large.

Power is failing and supply lines are uncertain in the *Godot* landscape too, its crafted indigence consonant with the background of both the war and its aftermath. The play is not 'about' the experience of war, any more than it is about any of the other myriad contexts and locations in which it has been performed over the ensuing decades. Nevertheless, a world in which Estragon gets beaten up by nameless aggressors, in which bare chicken bones are pounced upon for food, in which carrots are rationed and eventually lacking, and in which individuals are haplessly caught up in queues for their own salvation is one that is hospitable to these kinds of resonance. Could Beckett have written *Godot* before the second World War? It might seem unlikely.

The names originally allocated to the wayfarers of *Godot* are themselves evocative of diaspora. The first old man was given the Jewish name Lévy, which was changed in the second act to Estragon, the French word for tarragon, that subtle and aromatic herb.[3] The Slavic name Vladimir has grandiose etymological origins ('regal'; 'ruling with fame'), ironically so in context, but it is also the name of a Russian saint who converted to Orthodoxy from paganism in the tenth century. 'Pozzo', while being Italian for 'a well', has an aptly (ex)plosive ring to it, especially in conjunction with the persecuted creature who bears the English name of Lucky. And given the latter's servile status, it seems apposite that the epithet is often given to a pet canine. As it happens, the first film to include the comedy duo Laurel and Hardy – often evoked in connection with the cross-talk routines of *Godot* – was called *The Lucky Dog*, in which the down-at-heel hero (Stan Laurel) teams up with a stray. A lobby card advertising the film shows three men recoiling in horror from the seated dog, whose jaws are clamped over a long, drooping stick of dynamite, in a shot redolent of Lucky holding the whip in his mouth under the gaze of the three surrounding men.

Aside from changes of name, there are extensive variants between the first manuscript and the text as published by Les Éditions de Minuit in 1952,[4] but the situational dynamic of two men undergoing two successive episodes of waiting, each of which is punctuated by the arrival of two further men, and each curtailed by a boy messenger who announces a postponement of the meeting with Godot, remained intact.[5]

Soaked in waiting, the play was itself subjected to prolonged periods of waiting. Although *Godot* was cautiously adopted by the French stage director Roger Blin in early 1950, nearly three years elapsed before the play received its first performance on 3 January 1953, after uncertainties about venue, financing and what was deemed to be an inconvenient absence of parts for women. Blin did in fact admire Beckett's earlier apprentice piece, the three-act *Eleutheria*.[6] However, the tiny Théâtre de Babylone which he had at his disposal was ill equipped to stage a play requiring two juxtaposed and independent performance areas and a cast of seventeen characters. Of the two plays, it was *Godot* that accommodated the practical constraints of a theatre with 220 seats, a stage twenty feet wide and a severely limited budget for actors. These exacting circumstances – the reality for many of the French post-war pocket theatres – were offset, however, by the enthusiasm and energy of Blin. In the run-up to the opening of *Godot*, a radio broadcast of an abridged version of the play was secured, and the consequent publicity was undoubtedly a factor in convincing the new managing director of Éditions de Minuit, Jérôme Lindon, to publish the work in the autumn of 1952.

In the course of rehearsals, many of which he attended, Beckett suggested cuts or rewordings. Some though not all of these were incorporated into the second French edition, which appeared later in the year. Thus a passage near the beginning of Act II – in which Vladimir, in some measure relieved to be reunited with Estragon after their night apart, describes an interplay between the darkness of shut eyes and the inner darkness that can coexist with open eyes – was omitted after the first edition, perhaps because of its abstract, conceptual bias. Blin's own approach was indeed concrete and extrovert, as might be expected of a director who was at this time better known as an actor. Now in his forties, close in age to Beckett, Blin had appeared in a succession of films and stage productions, and was closely involved with the theatrical life of the capital. Turning to *Godot*, he paid particular attention to stage images, to the physical attributes of the actors and to the pattern of their movements, while striving at the same time to bring out the poetry of the text.

When *Godot* finally opened, textual considerations would have receded before the general bafflement with which the play was received, the unresponsive silences, the early departures from the auditorium. Support quickly rallied, however, bolstered by the positive reviews of such influential intellectuals as Jean Anouilh, Alain Robbe-Grillet, and Jacques Audiberti. Some noisy disagreement persisted, but the play survived to enjoy the success of notoriety and, accordingly, a buoyant first run.

A similarly stepped reaction greeted the London premiere, at the Arts Theatre Club, directed by the twenty-four-old Peter Hall in August 1955. In this case it was influential theatre critics such as Kenneth Tynan and Harold Hobson, in the *Observer* and the *Sunday Times*, who cut through the hostile initial reviews to champion the play in emphatic terms and reshape its reception. *Godot* had been translated into English fairly rapidly by Beckett in 1953, in response to requests from theatres, and was first published in America, by Grove Press, in 1954. At its English-language premiere in 1955, however, the play had not benefited from a pre-production radio broadcast, as had been the case in France.[7] And there were other hurdles to overcome. In England, the Office of the Lord Chamberlain was required to approve all plays intended for public performance.[8] Since the process of licence-granting erred on the side of conservatism, a preferred route for more provocative, avant-garde works was that of performance in establishments designated as private clubs (though these could also in principle be subjected to the attentions of the Lord Chamberlain's Office).

It was foreseeable that certain passages of *Godot* would fall foul of the Lord Chamberlain's blue pencil. These included moments deemed to contain unacceptable religious or sexual content, such as the exchange towards the end of Act 1 where Estragon talks of comparing himself to Christ, and observes that, in the region where Christ lived, 'they crucified quick.' Another casualty was the opening of Lucky's monologue, with its supposedly blasphemous description of 'a personal God quaquaquaqua with white beard quaquaquaqua outside time without extension who from the heights of divine apathia divine athambia divine aphasia loves us dearly with some exceptions', and so on. These deletions were restored when the first perform-ance took place in the 'private' space of the Arts Theatre Club, where another forfeited line, Vladimir's punning comment on the effect of hanging, 'It'd give us an erection', was able to achieve its full resonance – the more so for some of the audience, given the intense and sustained national coverage just three weeks earlier of the judicial execution by hanging, at Holloway Prison in London, of the young and glamorous Ruth Ellis. The last woman hanged in Britain, Ellis had been convicted of murdering her lover, and the grim ceremonial of her death was accompanied by vigils and protests outside the gaol.

It should be remembered too that *suicide* by hanging was still a criminal offence in Britain at this time.[9] Those who tried but failed to hang themselves – a very real prospect for Estragon and Vladimir, who have only a fragile bough and a rotting belt with which to attempt their suspension – could find themselves prosecuted and imprisoned as a result. It is in this context that the withering critical assessment of Peter Woodthorpe's Estragon, in the Theatre Review section of *The Times* on the morning after the first night, can be better understood: 'a whimpering grotesque, all for deserting or suicide by hanging'.[10] Even if suicide now elicits a more compassionate response, military desertion still attracts severe penalties. With such a range of religious, moral, sexual, ethical and judicial norms then thought vulnerable to corruption, the extent of the deletions to Beckett's text, which had to be reimposed when the production moved to the Criterion Theatre in September, were both infuriating to the author and of consequence for his carefully wrought text. As he wrote of the Lord Chamberlain to Barney Rosset on 21 April 1954: 'His incriminations are so preposterous that I'm afraid the whole thing is off. [. . .] The things I had expected and which I was half prepared to amend (reluctantly), but also passages that are vital to the play [. . .] and impossible either to alter or suppress.'[11]

It was the bowdlerised text that provided the basis for the first UK edition of the play, published by Faber the following year. This edition also differed in numerous small ways from its American counterpart, published two years earlier by Grove Press. Thus in the episode where Estragon requests money from Pozzo, Grove retains French currency – 'ten francs', followed by 'Even five' – while the first Faber edition has 'a shilling', followed by 'sixpence'. Earlier, the humorous reference to the English (as opposed to Irish) pronunciation of the word 'calm' is ethnically precise in Grove – 'The English say cawm' – but more consciously sardonic in Faber's 'All the best people say cawm.' Ten years on, in 1965, Faber published 'the complete and unexpurgated' *Godot* in a second edition.[12]

The parallel readings offered by the Faber bilingual edition published to mark the centenary of Beckett's birth fifty years later (*Waiting for Godot/En attendant Godot*, 2006) are a rich resource for those wishing to follow the fascinating complex of Beckettian practices that go under the general heading of 'translation'. At their broadest, these are concerned to form a tissue of references which work loosely together within their own linguistic and cultural frame, rather than translating a different and antecedent 'original'. Thus, in Lucky's speech, where the French cites the period 'depuis la mort de Voltaire' ('since the death of Voltaire'), the English prefers 'since the death of Bishop Berkeley'. The disparity of the interval – Voltaire dying in 1778, the Irish philosopher Berkeley in 1753 – is immaterial.

Similarly, in respect of naming, structurally similar names are chosen that can nevertheless be put to work in locally referential ways. The authority cited by the French Lucky, 'Conard', not only proposes itself as a legitimate French surname (held, for example, by a prominent publisher of the time, Louis Conard), but is also a homophone of the slang *connard*, meaning 'silly bugger' or 'damn fool'. The English Lucky, on the other hand, quotes 'Cunard', a name that creates a comparable yet distinct manifold of associations. While the first three letters similarly suggest offence to their bearer, the name also evokes Sir Samuel Cunard, founder of the prestigious Cunard Steamship Company, which ran between Britain and America, and his great-granddaughter, Nancy Cunard, a close friend of Beckett from his early years in Paris.

In the various afterlives of the text of *Godot*, significant changes were implemented by Beckett, notably when he directed the German production for the Schiller-Theater in Berlin in 1975; he would subsequently retain most of these changes when working with Walter Asmus on the latter's small English-language production with the San Quentin Drama Workshop in 1984. These modifications and Beckett's long-standing creative engagement with the play are fully documented in the *Theatrical Notebooks* edition of *Waiting for Godot*,[13] which draws on a range of production materials, including working notebooks and annotated copies used by Beckett. The process of revision involved verbal changes but also changes to movements (the excision of Pozzo's pipe-smoking), positions, gestures and images. Over the course of time Beckett also made occasional additions to the English text to align it more closely with the French. A notable example is the exchange in Act I, where Vladimir tries to maintain Estragon's commitment to the business of waiting by picturing the warm, hay-filled loft that they might occupy if taken under Godot's wing: 'All snug and dry, our bellies full, in the hay. That's worth waiting for, no?' This image, which was present in the French text from the beginning, was omitted from the English and American texts for over thirty years, until restored during the course of Beckett's collaboration with Asmus.[14]

Over the six decades since its first performance, *Godot* has been staged on countless occasions and in radically contrasting circumstances, whether by convicts in California's San Quentin Prison in 1957, or in war-torn Sarajevo in 1993, or by survivors of Hurricane Katrina in an open-air production in New Orleans in 2007. It may justifiably be claimed that the play's central figure – albeit absent, and possibly non-existent – has by now assumed his own existence, independent of both play and author. Godot is a 'pop culture ghost',[15] materialising in a huge variety of cultural and commercial contexts. There is a rich Godot cartoon tradition, and job advertisements or car insurance dealers routinely enjoin readers not to carry on 'waiting for Godot' but to apply immediately. Despite his non-appearance, Godot has passed into idiom.

Pozzo's stutter of uncertainty – 'I myself in your situation, if I had an appointment with a Godin . . . Godet . . . Godot . . . anyhow, you see who I mean, I'd wait till it was black night before I gave up' – is striking in that it combines a threatened sense of Godot's importance with an airy vagueness about his name, succeeding only on the third attempt. All the names have an identical first syllable, 'God', and some commentators have argued either that the play is a modern morality tale, a dramatisation of mankind's need – however unspoken – for a 'God'; or alternatively a post-theistic play, illustrating either His/Her factitiousness, or His/Her aloofness from the travails of the created order.

Waiting is certainly a well-established concept within a number of faiths, including Christianity, but normally involves a good measure of willed anticipation and optimism. The deferred gratification represented by Godot, by contrast, is no more secure, no more imminent, by the end of the play than it is at the beginning. The only surety is the renewability of waiting. Moreover, *En attendant Godot* was written originally in French, a language in which *god-*, far from having theological associations, prefixes a range of words denoting material objects, such as *godemiché* [dildo], or slang usages (*godasse* and *godillot* [shoe; clodhopper], *godiche* [ninny]). The second of Pozzo's tryouts – 'Godet' – means a goblet or pot, and is used colloquially in *prendre un godet* [to have a jar]. These earthy, homely words are just as consonant with Vladimir and Estragon's physical extension as any spiritual referent intended to endorse their occasional glances towards the metaphysical.

Other explanations have linked Godot with homophonic Godeau, a character in Balzac's little-known play *Le Faiseur* who is cited but who never appears, or a former racing cyclist, Roger Godeau, who is reported to have been keenly awaited at races by autograph hunters. Another attractive theory holds that the name derives from the last word of both of the play's acts – 'Let's go' – where the word 'go' leads not to departure but to immobility, summed up in the ensuing 'dot', full stop, period, so that the closure of each day remains impregnated by the evocation of Go-dot. Again, however, the association is available only in English, and then only as a product of reading. There is no punctuation on the stage – only pause and rhythm. What the lone figures are left with at the close of each act is something other than closure.

Beckett himself of course refused, resolutely and consistently, to supply excuses or explanations for his absent protagonist. A more profitable approach lies in simply acknowledging the happy phonetic genius of the name. It is as pleasing a find for Beckett as Figaro was for Beaumarchais. One might even argue that, in concluding with a vowel sound (like that equally compelling name, Dracula, which was not its author's first choice), the bearer's identity is left open, accorded indeterminate duration. Godot, taken on his own terms, is an unknown and possibly unknowable referent. A more satisfactory question than 'Who is he?' is 'Why is he needed?'

Godot's attributes shift, in the play, according to the needs of others. At times, his role seems potentially to be one of supplying material needs (money, shelter, provender). In a rare moment of solitude,[16] Vladimir sings a song about a dog who is beaten to death by a cook for stealing a crust of bread. A little later, when Estragon arrives, it is evident that he too has been beaten overnight by nameless assailants, perhaps for a similar crime. In the course of the play, available food becomes depleted. In Act I, Estragon eats and enjoys what he knows to be the last carrot. In Act II, only turnips and a blackened radish are left.

On the other hand, Vladimir and Estragon are full of questions (as is the play itself, in which interrogation far outweighs statement), surprisingly few of which relate to material concerns. Overwhelmingly, their questions reflect fundamental uncertainty – about their environment, their place in it, their future prospects. Perhaps this is why the play has proved so durable and so adaptable to changing times and conditions. At the time of writing, a new production starring Sir Ian McKellen as Estragon is touring Britain. Its reception has focused upon the play's relevance to current debate about resources, recession, financial rectitude and the fate of capital. '*Waiting for Godot* seems to have a unique resonance during times of social and political crisis. [. . .] Now it resonates again [. . .]. Consumerism is on the retreat. [. . .] It is a moment for introspection and stripping down to bare essentials. There is no drama more stripped down and essential than *Godot*.'[17] The meanings of *Godot*, and of its absent protagonist, seem set to continue evolving alongside us, for the unforeseeable future.

Notes

1 Cf. Colin Duckworth (ed.), *En attendant Godot* (London: Harrap, 1966), p. xlv.
2 Kenneth Tynan, *The Observer*, 7 August 1955.
3 Might one have expected Estragon to become Tarragon in translation? No, since it was not Beckett's practice to translate names when he translated his work. It is likely that he encountered the herb first in France, where it was commonly used in traditional recipes at a time when it remained uncommon in the UK and Ireland.
4 Cf. Colin Duckworth's edition of the play.
5 Ruby Cohn, *A Beckett Canon* (Ann Arbor, Mich.: University of Michigan Press, 2001), pp. 176–81.
6 Written in 1947, the play was withheld by Beckett, and remained unpublished until after his death.
7 The BBC had considered the idea of broadcasting *Godot* in 1953 but had not proceeded with it.
8 Although the Office of the Royal Chamberlain still exists to deal with matters pertaining to royal protocol, the role of theatrical jurisdiction or censorship was abolished in 1968.
9 Suicide was not decriminalised until 1961 in Britain, and not until 1993 in Ireland.
10 *The Times*, Thursday, 4 August 1955.
11 See James Knowlson, *Damned to Fame: The Life of Samuel Beckett* (London: Bloomsbury, 1996), p. 412.
12 This bowdlerised version was not eradicated, but returned to haunt the publishing history of *Godot*. When, in honour of Beckett's eightieth birthday in 1986, the *Complete Dramatic Works* was published by Faber, the text of *Godot* had unfathomably reverted to its censored 1956 version; it was corrected in the paperback edition.
13 Dougald McMillan and James Knowlson (eds.), *The Theatrical Notebooks of Samuel Beckett*, vol. I: *Waiting for Godot* (London: Faber and Faber, 1993).
14 McMillan and Knowlson, *Theatrical Notebooks*, p. xv.
15 Kim Newman, interviewed about his 1992 horror novel *Anno Dracula*: 'Dracula exists in a very real sense, in that he's a kind of pop-culture ghost. He exists in the same sense as Sherlock Holmes [. . .]. Any character who enters popular culture has a genuine existence, independent of the work in which they appeared. Dracula no longer belongs to Bram Stoker [. . .].

[He] has escaped from his text' (*Open Book*, BBC Radio 4, 22 January 2009).

16 In his Berlin and San Quentin productions Beckett included Estragon on stage at the start of Act II, observing the singing Vladimir and providing a parallel to the co-presence of both men at the start of Act I (McMillan and Knowlson, *Theatrical Notebooks*, p. xiii)

17 David Smith, 'In Godot We Trust', *The Observer*, Review section, 8 March 2009.

Table of Dates

Where unspecified, translations from French to English or vice versa are by Beckett.

1906

13 April   Samuel Beckett [Samuel Barclay Beckett] born in 'Cooldrinagh', a house in Foxrock, a village south of Dublin, on Good Friday, the second child of William Beckett and May Beckett, née Roe; he is preceded by a brother, Frank Edward, born 26 July 1902.

1911

                Enters kindergarten at Ida and Pauline Elsner's private academy in Leopardstown.

1915

                Attends larger Earlsfort House School in Dublin.

1920

                Follows Frank to Portora Royal, a distinguished Protestant boarding school in Enniskillen, County Fermanagh (soon to become part of Northern Ireland).

1923

October   Enrols at Trinity College Dublin (TCD) to study for an Arts degree.

1926

August   First visit to France, a month-long cycling tour of the Loire Valley.

1927

April–August   Travels through Florence and Venice, visiting museums, galleries and churches.

December   Receives BA in Modern Languages (French and Italian) and graduates first in the First Class.

1928

Jan.–June Teaches French and English at Campbell College, Belfast.

September First trip to Germany to visit seventeen-year-old Peggy Sinclair, a cousin on his father's side, and her family in Kassel.

1 November Arrives in Paris as an exchange *lecteur* at the École Normale Supérieure. Quickly becomes friends with his predecessor, Thomas McGreevy [after 1943, MacGreevy], who introduces Beckett to James Joyce and other influential anglophone writers and publishers.

December Spends Christmas in Kassel (as also in 1929, 1930 and 1931).

1929

June Publishes first critical essay ('Dante . . . Bruno . Vico . . Joyce') and first story ('Assumption') in *transition* magazine.

1930

July *Whoroscope* (Paris: Hours Press).

October Returns to TCD to begin a two-year appointment as lecturer in French.

November Introduced by MacGreevy to the painter and writer Jack B. Yeats in Dublin.

1931

March *Proust* (London: Chatto & Windus).

September First Irish publication, the poem 'Alba' in *Dublin Magazine*.

1932

January Resigns his lectureship via telegram from Kassel and moves to Paris.

Feb.–June First serious attempt at a novel, the posthumously published *Dream of Fair to Middling Women*.

December Story 'Dante and the Lobster' appears in *This Quarter* (Paris).

1933

3 May — Death of Peggy Sinclair from tuberculosis.

26 June — Death of William Beckett from a heart attack.

1934

January — Moves to London and begins psychoanalysis with Wilfred Bion at the Tavistock Clinic.

February — *Negro Anthology*, edited by Nancy Cunard and with numerous translations by Beckett from the French (London: Wishart & Co.).

May — *More Pricks Than Kicks* (London: Chatto & Windus).

Aug.–Sept. — Contributes several stories and reviews to literary magazines in London and Dublin.

1935

November — *Echo's Bones and Other Precipitates*, a cycle of thirteen poems (Paris: Europa Press).

1936

Returns to Dublin.

29 September — Leaves Ireland for a seven-month stay in Germany.

1937

Apr.–Aug. — First serious attempt at a play, *Human Wishes*, about Samuel Johnson and his household.

October — Settles in Paris.

1938

6/7 January — Stabbed by a street pimp in Montparnasse. Among his visitors at Hôpital Broussais is Suzanne Deschevaux-Dumesnil, an acquaintance who is to become Beckett's companion for life.

March — *Murphy* (London: Routledge).

April — Begins writing poetry directly in French.

1939

3 September — Great Britain and France declare war on Germany. Beckett abruptly ends a visit to Ireland and returns to Paris the next day.

1940

June — Travels south with Suzanne following the Fall of France, as part of the exodus from the capital.

September — Returns to Paris.

1941

13 January — Death of James Joyce in Zurich.

1 September — Joins the Resistance cell Gloria SMH.

1942

16 August — Goes into hiding with Suzanne after the arrest of close friend Alfred Péron.

6 October — Arrival at Roussillon, a small village in unoccupied southern France.

1944

24 August — Liberation of Paris.

1945

30 March — Awarded the Croix de Guerre.

Aug.–Dec. — Volunteers as a storekeeper and interpreter with the Irish Red Cross in Saint-Lô, Normandy.

1946

July — Publishes first fiction in French – a truncated version of the short story 'Suite' (later to become 'La Fin') in *Les Temps modernes*, owing to a misunderstanding by editors – as well as a critical essay on Dutch painters Geer and Bram van Velde in *Cahiers d'art*.

1947

Jan.–Feb. — Writes first play, in French, *Eleutheria* (published posthumously).

April — *Murphy*, French translation (Paris: Bordas).

1948

Undertakes a number of translations commissioned by UNESCO and by Georges Duthuit.

1950

25 August   Death of May Beckett.

1951

March   *Molloy*, in French (Paris: Les Éditions de
                     Minuit).

November   *Malone meurt* (Paris: Minuit).

1952

                     Purchases land at Ussy-sur-Marne,
                     subsequently Beckett's preferred location for
                     writing.

September   *En attendant Godot* (Paris: Minuit).

1953

5 January   Premiere of *Godot* at the Théâtre de Babylone
                     in Montparnasse, directed by Roger Blin.

May   *L'Innommable* (Paris: Minuit).

August   *Watt*, in English (Paris: Olympia Press).

1954

8 September   *Waiting for Godot* (New York: Grove Press).

13 September   Death of Frank Beckett from lung cancer.

1955

March   *Molloy*, translated into English with Patrick
                     Bowles (New York: Grove; Paris: Olympia).

3 August   First English production of *Godot* opens in
                     London at the Arts Theatre.

November   *Nouvelles et Textes pour rien* (Paris: Minuit).

1956

3 January   American *Godot* premiere in Miami.

February   First British publication of *Waiting for Godot*
                     (London: Faber).

October   *Malone Dies* (New York: Grove).

1957

January   First radio broadcast, *All That Fall* on the
                     BBC Third Programme.
                     Fin de partie, suivi de Acte sans paroles (Paris:
                     Minuit).

28 March   Death of Jack B. Yeats.

TABLE OF DATES

August	*All That Fall* (London: Faber).
October	*Tous ceux qui tombent*, translation of *All That Fall* with Robert Pinget (Paris: Minuit).
1958	
April	*Endgame*, translation of *Fin de partie* (London: Faber).
	From an Abandoned Work (London: Faber).
July	*Krapp's Last Tape* in Grove Press's literary magazine, *Evergreen Review*.
September	*The Unnamable* (New York: Grove).
December	*Anthology of Mexican Poetry*, translated by Beckett (Bloomington, Ind.: Indiana University Press; later reprinted in London by Thames & Hudson).
1959	
March	*La Dernière bande*, translation of *Krapp's Last Tape* with Pierre Leyris, in the Parisian literary magazine *Les Lettres nouvelles*.
2 July	Receives honorary D.Litt. degree from Trinity College Dublin.
November	*Embers* in *Evergreen Review*.
December	*Cendres*, translation of *Embers* with Pinget, in *Les Lettres nouvelles*.
	Three Novels: Molloy, Malone Dies, The Unnamable (New York: Grove; Paris: Olympia Press).
1961	
January	*Comment c'est* (Paris: Minuit).
24 March	Marries Suzanne at Folkestone, Kent.
May	Shares Prix International des Editeurs with Jorge Luis Borges.
August	*Poems in English* (London: Calder).
September	*Happy Days* (New York: Grove).
1963	
February	*Oh les beaux jours*, translation of *Happy Days* (Paris: Minuit).

xxiv

May	Assists with the German production of *Play* (*Spiel*, translated by Elmar and Erika Tophoven) in Ulm.
22 May	Outline of *Film* sent to Grove Press. *Film* would be produced in 1964, starring Buster Keaton, and released at the Venice Film Festival the following year.
1964	
March	*Play and Two Short Pieces for Radio* (London: Faber).
April	*How It Is*, translation of *Comment c'est* (London: Calder; New York: Grove).
June	*Comédie*, translation of *Play*, in *Les Lettres nouvelles*.
July–Aug.	First and only trip to the United States, to assist with the production of *Film* in New York.
1965	
October	*Imagination morte imaginez* (Paris: Minuit).
November	*Imagination Dead Imagine* (London: *The Sunday Times*; Calder).
1966	
January	*Comédie et Actes divers*, including *Dis Joe* and *Va et vient* (Paris: Minuit).
February	*Assez* (Paris: Minuit).
October	*Bing* (Paris: Minuit).
1967	
February	*D'un ouvrage abandonné* (Paris: Minuit). *Têtes-mortes* (Paris: Minuit).
16 March	Death of Thomas MacGreevy.
June	*Eh Joe and Other Writings*, including *Act Without Words II* and *Film* (London: Faber).
July	*Come and Go*, English translation of *Va et vient* (London: Calder).
26 September	Directs first solo production, *Endspiel* (translation of *Endgame* by Elmar Tophoven) in Berlin.

Court Theatre in honour of Beckett's
seventieth birthday.

Autumn   *All Strange Away*, illustrated with etchings by
Edward Gorey (New York: Gotham Book
Mart).

Foirades/Fizzles, in French and English,
illustrated with etchings by Jasper Johns (New
York: Petersburg Press).

December   *Footfalls* (London: Faber).

1977

March   *Collected Poems in English and French* (London:
Calder; New York: Grove).

1978

May   *Pas*, translation of *Footfalls* (Paris: Minuit).

August   *Poèmes, suivi de mirlitonnades* (Paris: Minuit).

1980

January   *Compagnie* (Paris: Minuit).
Company (London: Calder).

May   Directs *Endgame* in London with Rick
Cluchey and the San Quentin Drama
Workshop.

1981

March   *Mal vu mal dit* (Paris: Minuit).

April   *Rockaby and Other Short Pieces* (New York:
Grove).

October   *Ill Seen Ill Said*, translation of *Mal vu mal dit*
(New York: *New Yorker*; Grove).

1983

April   *Worstward Ho* (London: Calder).

September   *Disjecta: Miscellaneous Writings and a
Dramatic Fragment*, containing critical
essays on art and literature as well as the
unfinished play *Human Wishes*
(London: Calder).

1984

February   Oversees San Quentin Drama Workshop

	production of *Godot*, directed by Walter Asmus, in London.
	Collected Shorter Plays (London: Faber; New York: Grove).
May	*Collected Poems, 1930–1978* (London: Calder).
July	*Collected Shorter Prose, 1945–1980* (London: Calder).

1989

April	*Stirrings Still*, with illustrations by Louis le Brocquy (New York: Blue Moon Books).
June	*Nohow On: Company, Ill Seen Ill Said, Worstward Ho*, illustrated with etchings by Robert Ryman (New York: Limited Editions Club).
17 July	Death of Suzanne Beckett.
22 December	Death of Samuel Beckett. Burial in Cimetière de Montparnasse.

★

1990

As the Story Was Told: Uncollected and Late Prose (London: Calder; New York: Riverrun Press).

1992

Dream of Fair to Middling Women (Dublin: Black Cat Press).

1995

Eleutheria (Paris: Minuit).

1996

Eleutheria, translated into English by Barbara Wright (London: Faber).

1998

No Author Better Served: The Correspondence of Samuel Beckett and Alan Schneider, edited by Maurice Harmon (Cambridge, Mass.: Harvard University Press).

2000

Beckett on Film: nineteen films, by different directors, of Beckett's works for the stage (RTÉ, Channel 4 and Irish Film Board; DVD, London: Clarence Pictures).

2006

Samuel Beckett: Works for Radio: The Original Broadcasts: five works spanning the period 1957–1976 (CD, London: British Library Board).

2009

The Letters of Samuel Beckett, 1929–1940, edited by Martha Dow Fehsenfeld and Lois More Overbeck (Cambridge: Cambridge University Press).

Compiled by Cassandra Nelson

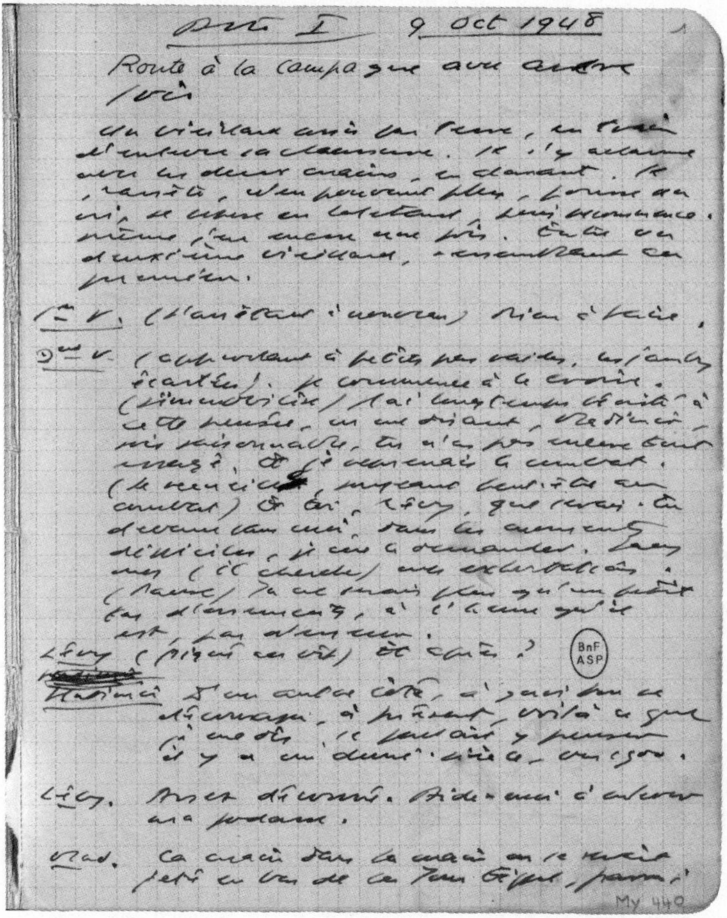
9 Oct 1948
Route à la campagne avec arbre
BnF
ASP
My 440

Manuscript of the opening page of *En attendant Godot* (*Waiting for Godot*)
Courtesy of the Bibliothèque nationale de France.
© The Estate of Samuel Beckett.

Waiting for Godot

The first performance in Great Britain of *Waiting for Godot* was given at the Arts Theatre, London, on 3 August 1955. It was directed by Peter Hall, and the decor was by Peter Snow. The cast was as follows:

ESTRAGON Peter Woodthorpe
VLADIMIR Paul Daneman
LUCKY Timothy Bateson
POZZO Peter Bull
A BOY Michael Walker

CAST

ESTRAGON
VLADIMIR
LUCKY
POZZO
A BOY

Act One

A country road. A tree. Evening.

ESTRAGON, *sitting on a low mound, is trying to take off his boot. He pulls at it with both hands, panting. He gives up, exhausted, rests, tries again. As before.*
Enter VLADIMIR.

ESTRAGON: [*Giving up again.*] Nothing to be done.

VLADIMIR: [*Advancing with short, stiff strides, legs wide apart.*] I'm beginning to come round to that opinion. All my life I've tried to put it from me, saying, Vladimir, be reasonable, you haven't yet tried everything. And I resumed the struggle. [*He broods, musing on the struggle. Turning to* ESTRAGON.] So there you are again.

ESTRAGON: Am I?

VLADIMIR: I'm glad to see you back. I thought you were gone for ever.

ESTRAGON: Me too.

VLADIMIR: Together again at last! We'll have to celebrate this. But how? [*He reflects.*] Get up till I embrace you.

ESTRAGON: [*Irritably.*] Not now, not now.

VLADIMIR: [*Hurt, coldly.*] May one enquire where His Highness spent the night?

ESTRAGON: In a ditch.

VLADIMIR: [*Admiringly.*] A ditch! Where?

ESTRAGON: [*Without gesture.*] Over there.

VLADIMIR: And they didn't beat you?

ESTRAGON: Beat me? Certainly they beat me.

VLADIMIR: The same lot as usual?

ESTRAGON: The same? I don't know.

VLADIMIR: When I think of it . . . all these years . . . but for me . . . where would you be . . . ? [*Decisively.*]

You'd be nothing more than a little heap of bones at the present minute, no doubt about it.

ESTRAGON: And what of it?

VLADIMIR: [*Gloomily.*] It's too much for one man. [*Pause. Cheerfully.*] On the other hand, what's the good of losing heart now, that's what I say. We should have thought of it a million years ago, in the nineties.

ESTRAGON: Ah, stop blathering and help me off with this bloody thing.

VLADIMIR: Hand in hand from the top of the Eiffel Tower, among the first. We were presentable in those days. Now it's too late. They wouldn't even let us up. [ESTRAGON *tears at his boot.*] What are you doing?

ESTRAGON: Taking off my boot. Did that never happen to you?

VLADIMIR: Boots must be taken off every day, I'm tired telling you that. Why don't you listen to me?

ESTRAGON: [*Feebly.*] Help me!

VLADIMIR: It hurts?

ESTRAGON: Hurts! He wants to know if it hurts!

VLADIMIR: [*Angrily.*] No one ever suffers but you. I don't count. I'd like to hear what you'd say if you had what I have.

ESTRAGON: It hurts?

VLADIMIR: Hurts! He wants to know if it hurts!

ESTRAGON: [*Pointing.*] You might button it all the same.

VLADIMIR: [*Stooping.*] True. [*He buttons his fly.*] Never neglect the little things of life.

ESTRAGON: What do you expect, you always wait till the last moment.

VLADIMIR: [*Musingly.*] The last moment . . . [*He meditates.*] Hope deferred maketh the something sick, who said that?

ESTRAGON: Why don't you help me?

VLADIMIR: Sometimes I feel it coming all the same. Then I go all queer. [*He takes off his hat, peers inside it, feels about inside it, shakes it, puts it on again.*] How shall I say? Relieved and at the same time . . . [*He searches for the word.*] . . . appalled. [*With emphasis.*] AP-PALLED. [*He takes off his hat again, peers inside it.*] Funny. [*He knocks on the crown as though to dislodge a foreign body, peers into it again, puts it on again.*] Nothing to be done. [ESTRAGON *with a supreme effort succeeds in pulling off his boot. He looks inside it, feels about inside it, turns it upside down, shakes it, looks on the ground to see if anything has fallen out, finds nothing, feels inside it again, staring sightlessly before him.*] Well?

ESTRAGON: Nothing.

VLADIMIR: Show.

ESTRAGON: There's nothing to show.

VLADIMIR: Try and put it on again.

ESTRAGON: [*Examining his foot.*] I'll air it for a bit.

VLADIMIR: There's man all over for you, blaming on his boots the faults of his feet. [*He takes off his hat again, peers inside it, feels about inside it, knocks on the crown, blows into it, puts it on again.*] This is getting alarming. [*Silence.* VLADIMIR *deep in thought,* ESTRAGON *pulling at his toes.*] One of the thieves was saved. [*Pause.*] It's a reasonable percentage. [*Pause.*] Gogo.

ESTRAGON: What?

VLADIMIR: Suppose we repented.

ESTRAGON: Repented what?

VLADIMIR: Oh . . . [*He reflects.*] We wouldn't have to go into the details.

ESTRAGON: Our being born?

[VLADIMIR *breaks into a hearty laugh which he immediately stifles, his hand pressed to his pubis, his face contorted.*]

VLADIMIR: One daren't even laugh any more.

ESTRAGON: Dreadful privation.

VLADIMIR: Merely smile. [*He smiles suddenly from ear to*

ear, keeps smiling, ceases as suddenly.] It's not the same thing. Nothing to be done. [*Pause.*] Gogo.

ESTRAGON: [*Irritably.*] What is it?

VLADIMIR: Did you ever read the Bible?

ESTRAGON: The Bible . . . [*He reflects.*] I must have taken a look at it.

VLADIMIR: Do you remember the Gospels?

ESTRAGON: I remember the maps of the Holy Land. Coloured they were. Very pretty. The Dead Sea was pale blue. The very look of it made me thirsty. That's where we'll go, I used to say, that's where we'll go for our honeymoon. We'll swim. We'll be happy.

VLADIMIR: You should have been a poet.

ESTRAGON: I was. [*Gesture towards his rags.*] Isn't that obvious.

[*Silence.*]

VLADIMIR: Where was I . . . How's your foot?

ESTRAGON: Swelling visibly.

VLADIMIR: Ah yes, the two thieves. Do you remember the story?

ESTRAGON: No.

VLADIMIR: Shall I tell it to you?

ESTRAGON: No.

VLADIMIR: It'll pass the time. [*Pause.*] Two thieves, crucified at the same time as our Saviour. One –

ESTRAGON: Our what?

VLADIMIR: Our Saviour. Two thieves. One is supposed to have been saved and the other . . . [*He searches for the contrary of saved*] . . . damned.

ESTRAGON: Saved from what?

VLADIMIR: Hell.

ESTRAGON: I'm going.

[*He does not move.*]

VLADIMIR: And yet . . . [*Pause.*] . . . how is it – this is not boring you I hope – how is it that of the four Evangelists only one speaks of a thief being saved.

The four of them were there – or thereabouts – and only one speaks of a thief being saved. [*Pause.*] Come on, Gogo, return the ball, can't you, once in a way?

ESTRAGON: [*With exaggerated enthusiasm.*] I find this really most extraordinarily interesting.

VLADIMIR: One out of four. Of the other three two don't mention any thieves at all and the third says that both of them abused him.

ESTRAGON: Who?

VLADIMIR: What?

ESTRAGON: What's all this about? Abused who?

VLADIMIR: The Saviour.

ESTRAGON: Why?

VLADIMIR: Because he wouldn't save them.

ESTRAGON: From hell?

VLADIMIR: Imbecile! From death.

ESTRAGON: I thought you said hell.

VLADIMIR: From death, from death.

ESTRAGON: Well, what of it?

VLADIMIR: Then the two of them must have been damned.

ESTRAGON: And why not?

VLADIMIR: But one of the four says that one of the two was saved.

ESTRAGON: Well? They don't agree, and that's all there is to it.

VLADIMIR: But all four were there. And only one speaks of a thief being saved. Why believe him rather than the others?

ESTRAGON: Who believes him?

VLADIMIR: Everybody. It's the only version they know.

ESTRAGON: People are bloody ignorant apes.

[*He rises painfully, goes limping to extreme left, halts, gazes into distance off with his hand screening his eyes, turns, goes to extreme right, gazes into distance.* VLADIMIR *watches him, then goes and picks up the boot, peers into it, drops it hastily.*]

9

VLADIMIR: Pah!

[*He spits.* ESTRAGON *moves to centre, halts with his back to auditorium.*]

ESTRAGON: Charming spot. [*He turns, advances to front, halts facing auditorium.*] Inspiring prospects. [*He turns to* VLADIMIR.] Let's go.

VLADIMIR: We can't.

ESTRAGON: Why not?

VLADIMIR: We're waiting for Godot.

ESTRAGON: [*Despairingly.*] Ah! [*Pause.*] You're sure it was here?

VLADIMIR: What?

ESTRAGON: That we were to wait.

VLADIMIR: He said by the tree. [*They look at the tree.*] Do you see any others?

ESTRAGON: What is it?

VLADIMIR: I don't know. A willow.

ESTRAGON: Where are the leaves?

VLADIMIR: It must be dead.

ESTRAGON: No more weeping.

VLADIMIR: Or perhaps it's not the season.

ESTRAGON: Looks to me more like a bush.

VLADIMIR: A shrub.

ESTRAGON: A bush.

VLADIMIR: A – . What are you insinuating? That we've come to the wrong place?

ESTRAGON: He should be here.

VLADIMIR: He didn't say for sure he'd come.

ESTRAGON: And if he doesn't come?

VLADIMIR: We'll come back tomorrow.

ESTRAGON: And then the day after tomorrow.

VLADIMIR: Possibly.

ESTRAGON: And so on.

VLADIMIR: The point is –

ESTRAGON: Until he comes.

VLADIMIR: You're merciless.

ESTRAGON: We came here yesterday.

VLADIMIR: Ah no, there you're mistaken.

ESTRAGON: What did we do yesterday?

VLADIMIR: What did we do yesterday?

ESTRAGON: Yes.

VLADIMIR: Why . . . [*Angrily.*] Nothing is certain when you're about.

ESTRAGON: In my opinion we were here.

VLADIMIR: [*Looking around.*] You recognize the place?

ESTRAGON: I didn't say that.

VLADIMIR: Well?

ESTRAGON: That makes no difference.

VLADIMIR: All the same . . . that tree . . . [*Turning towards the auditorium*] . . . that bog.

ESTRAGON: You're sure it was this evening?

VLADIMIR: What?

ESTRAGON: That we were to wait.

VLADIMIR: He said Saturday. [*Pause.*] I think.

ESTRAGON: You think.

VLADIMIR: I must have made a note of it.
[*He fumbles in his pockets, bursting with miscellaneous rubbish.*]

ESTRAGON: [*Very insidious.*] But what Saturday? And is it Saturday? Is it not rather Sunday? [*Pause.*] Or Monday? [*Pause.*] Or Friday?

VLADIMIR: [*Looking wildly about him, as though the date was inscribed in the landscape.*] It's not possible!

ESTRAGON: Or Thursday?

VLADIMIR: What'll we do?

ESTRAGON: If he came yesterday and we weren't here you may be sure he won't come again today.

VLADIMIR: But you say we were here yesterday.

ESTRAGON: I may be mistaken. [*Pause.*] Let's stop talking for a minute, do you mind?

VLADIMIR: [*Feebly.*] All right. [ESTRAGON *sits down on the mound.* VLADIMIR *paces agitatedly to and fro,*

11

halting from time to time to gaze into the distance off.
ESTRAGON *falls asleep.* VLADIMIR *halts before*
ESTRAGON.] Gogo! . . . Gogo! . . . GOGO!
[ESTRAGON *wakes with a start.*]

ESTRAGON: [*Restored to the horror of his situation.*] I
was asleep! [*Despairingly.*] Why will you never let me
sleep?

VLADIMIR: I felt lonely.

ESTRAGON: I had a dream.

VLADIMIR: Don't tell me!

ESTRAGON: I dreamt that –

VLADIMIR: DON'T TELL ME!

ESTRAGON: [*Gesture towards the universe.*] This one is
enough for you? [*Silence.*] It's not nice of you, Didi.
Who am I to tell my private nightmares to if I can't
tell them to you?

VLADIMIR: Let them remain private. You know I can't
bear that.

ESTRAGON: [*Coldly.*] There are times when I wonder if it
wouldn't be better for us to part.

VLADIMIR: You wouldn't go far.

ESTRAGON: That would be too bad, really too bad.
[*Pause.*] Wouldn't it, Didi, be really too bad? [*Pause.*]
When you think of the beauty of the way. [*Pause.*] And
the goodness of the wayfarers. [*Pause. Wheedling.*]
Wouldn't it, Didi?

VLADIMIR: Calm yourself.

ESTRAGON: [*Voluptuously.*] Calm . . . calm . . . The
English say cawm. [*Pause.*] You know the story of the
Englishman in the brothel?

VLADIMIR: Yes.

ESTRAGON: Tell it to me.

VLADIMIR: Ah, stop it!

ESTRAGON: An Englishman having drunk a little more than
usual goes to a brothel. The bawd asks him if he wants
a fair one, a dark one, or a red-haired one. Go on.

VLADIMIR: STOP IT!

[*Exit* VLADIMIR *hurriedly.* ESTRAGON *gets up and follows him as far as the limit of the stage. Gestures of* ESTRAGON *like those of a spectator encouraging a pugilist. Enter* VLADIMIR. *He brushes past* ESTRAGON, *crosses the stage with bowed head.* ESTRAGON *takes a step towards him, halts.*]

ESTRAGON: [*Gently.*] You wanted to speak to me? [*Silence.* ESTRAGON *takes a step forward.*] You had something to say to me? [*Silence. Another step forward.*] Didi . . .

VLADIMIR: [*Without turning.*] I've nothing to say to you.

ESTRAGON: [*Step forward.*] You're angry? [*Silence. Step forward.*] Forgive me. [*Silence. Step forward.* ESTRAGON *lays his hand on* VLADIMIR*'s shoulder.*] Come, Didi. [*Silence.*] Give me your hand. [VLADIMIR *half turns.*] Embrace me! [VLADIMIR *stiffens.*] Don't be stubborn! [VLADIMIR *softens. They embrace.* ESTRAGON *recoils.*] You stink of garlic!

VLADIMIR: It's for the kidneys. [*Silence.* ESTRAGON *looks attentively at the tree.*] What do we do now?

ESTRAGON: Wait.

VLADIMIR: Yes, but while waiting.

ESTRAGON: What about hanging ourselves?

VLADIMIR: Hmm. It'd give us an erection!

ESTRAGON: [*Highly excited.*] An erection!

VLADIMIR: With all that follows. Where it falls, mandrakes grow. That's why they shriek when you pull them up. Did you not know that?

ESTRAGON: Let's hang ourselves immediately!

VLADIMIR: From a bough? [*They go towards the tree.*] I wouldn't trust it.

ESTRAGON: We can always try.

VLADIMIR: Go ahead.

ESTRAGON: After you.

VLADIMIR: No no, you first.

ESTRAGON: Why me?

VLADIMIR: You're lighter than I am.

ESTRAGON: Just so!

VLADIMIR: I don't understand.

ESTRAGON: Use your intelligence, can't you?

[VLADIMIR *uses his intelligence.*]

VLADIMIR: [*Finally.*] I remain in the dark.

ESTRAGON: This is how it is. [*He reflects.*] The bough . . .
the bough . . . [*Angrily.*] Use your head, can't you?

VLADIMIR: You're my only hope.

ESTRAGON: [*With effort.*] Gogo light – bough not break –
Gogo dead. Didi heavy – bough break – Didi alone.
Whereas –

VLADIMIR: I hadn't thought of that.

ESTRAGON: If it hangs you it'll hang anything.

VLADIMIR: But am I heavier than you?

ESTRAGON: So you tell me. I don't know. There's an even
chance. Or nearly.

VLADIMIR: Well? What do we do?

ESTRAGON: Don't let's do anything. It's safer.

VLADIMIR: Let's wait and see what he says.

ESTRAGON: Who?

VLADIMIR: Godot.

ESTRAGON: Good idea.

VLADIMIR: Let's wait till we know exactly how we stand.

ESTRAGON: On the other hand, it might be better to
strike the iron before it freezes.

VLADIMIR: I'm curious to hear what he has to offer. Then
we'll take it or leave it.

ESTRAGON: What exactly did we ask him for?

VLADIMIR: Were you not there?

ESTRAGON: I can't have been listening.

VLADIMIR: Oh . . . nothing very definite.

ESTRAGON: A kind of prayer.

VLADIMIR: Precisely.

ESTRAGON: A vague supplication.

VLADIMIR: Exactly.

ESTRAGON: And what did he reply?

VLADIMIR: That he'd see.

ESTRAGON: That he couldn't promise anything.

VLADIMIR: That he'd have to think it over.

ESTRAGON: In the quiet of his home.

VLADIMIR: Consult his family.

ESTRAGON: His friends.

VLADIMIR: His agents.

ESTRAGON: His correspondents.

VLADIMIR: His books.

ESTRAGON: His bank account.

VLADIMIR: Before taking a decision.

ESTRAGON: It's the normal thing.

VLADIMIR: Is it not?

ESTRAGON: I think it is.

VLADIMIR: I think so too.

[Silence.]

ESTRAGON: [Anxious.] And we?

VLADIMIR: I beg your pardon?

ESTRAGON: I said, And we?

VLADIMIR: I don't understand.

ESTRAGON: Where do we come in?

VLADIMIR: Come in?

ESTRAGON: Take your time.

VLADIMIR: Come in? On our hands and knees.

ESTRAGON: As bad as that?

VLADIMIR: Your Worship wishes to assert his prerogatives?

ESTRAGON: We've no rights any more?

[Laugh of VLADIMIR, stifled as before, less the smile.]

VLADIMIR: You'd make me laugh, if it wasn't prohibited.

ESTRAGON: We've lost our rights?

VLADIMIR: [Distinctly.] We got rid of them.

[Silence. They remain motionless, arms dangling, heads sunk, sagging at the knees.]

ESTRAGON: [*Feebly.*] We're not tied? [*Pause.*] We're not –
VLADIMIR: Listen!
 [*They listen, grotesquely rigid.*]
ESTRAGON: I hear nothing.
VLADIMIR: Hssst! [*They listen.* ESTRAGON *loses his balance, almost falls. He clutches the arm of* VLADIMIR, *who totters. They listen, huddled together.*] Nor I. [*Sighs of relief. They relax and separate.*]
ESTRAGON: You gave me a fright.
VLADIMIR: I thought it was he.
ESTRAGON: Who?
VLADIMIR: Godot.
ESTRAGON: Pah! The wind in the reeds.
VLADIMIR: I could have sworn I heard shouts.
ESTRAGON: And why would he shout?
VLADIMIR: At his horse.
 [*Silence.*]
ESTRAGON: [*Violently.*] I'm hungry.
VLADIMIR: Do you want a carrot?
ESTRAGON: Is that all there is?
VLADIMIR: I might have some turnips.
ESTRAGON: Give me a carrot. [VLADIMIR *rummages in his pockets, takes out a turnip and gives it to* ESTRAGON *who takes a bite out of it. Angrily.*] It's a turnip!
VLADIMIR: Oh pardon! I could have sworn it was a carrot. [*He rummages again in his pockets, finds nothing but turnips.*] All that's turnips. [*He rummages.*] You must have eaten the last. [*He rummages.*] Wait, I have it. [*He brings out a carrot and gives it to* ESTRAGON.] There, dear fellow. [ESTRAGON *wipes the carrot on his sleeve and begins to eat it.*] Give me the turnip. [ESTRAGON *gives back the turnip which* VLADIMIR *puts in his pocket.*] Make it last, that's the end of them.

ESTRAGON: [*Chewing.*] I asked you a question.

VLADIMIR: Ah.

ESTRAGON: Did you reply?

VLADIMIR: How's the carrot?

ESTRAGON: It's a carrot.

VLADIMIR: So much the better, so much the better.
[*Pause.*] What was it you wanted to know?

ESTRAGON: I've forgotten. [*Chews.*] That's what annoys
me. [*He looks at the carrot appreciatively, dangles it
between finger and thumb.*] I'll never forget this
carrot. [*He sucks the end of it meditatively.*] Ah yes,
now I remember.

VLADIMIR: Well?

ESTRAGON: [*His mouth full, vacuously.*] We're not tied!

VLADIMIR: I don't hear a word you're saying.

ESTRAGON: [*Chews, swallows.*] I'm asking you if we're
tied.

VLADIMIR: Tied?

ESTRAGON: Ti-ed.

VLADIMIR: How do you mean, tied?

ESTRAGON: Down.

VLADIMIR: But to whom. By whom?

ESTRAGON: To your man.

VLADIMIR: To Godot? Tied to Godot? What an idea! No
question of it. [*Pause.*] For the moment.

ESTRAGON: His name is Godot?

VLADIMIR: I think so.

ESTRAGON: Fancy that. [*He raises what remains of the
carrot by the stub of leaf, twirls it before his eyes.*]
Funny, the more you eat the worse it gets.

VLADIMIR: With me it's just the opposite.

ESTRAGON: In other words?

VLADIMIR: I get used to the muck as I go along.

ESTRAGON: [*After prolonged reflection.*] Is that the
opposite?

VLADIMIR: Question of temperament.

ESTRAGON: Of character.

VLADIMIR: Nothing you can do about it.

ESTRAGON: No use struggling.

VLADIMIR: One is what one is.

ESTRAGON: No use wriggling.

VLADIMIR: The essential doesn't change.

ESTRAGON: Nothing to be done. [*He proffers the remains of the carrot to* VLADIMIR.] Like to finish it?
[*A terrible cry, close at hand.* ESTRAGON *drops the carrot. They remain motionless, then together make a sudden rush towards the wings.* ESTRAGON *stops half-way, runs back, picks up the carrot, stuffs it in his pocket, runs towards* VLADIMIR *who is waiting for him, stops again, runs back, picks up his boot, runs to rejoin* VLADIMIR. *Huddled together, shoulders hunched, cringing away from the menace, they wait.*
Enter POZZO *and* LUCKY. POZZO *drives* LUCKY *by means of a rope passed round his neck, so that* LUCKY *is the first to appear, followed by the rope, which is long enough to allow him to reach the middle of the stage before* POZZO *appears.* LUCKY *carries a heavy bag, a folding stool, a picnic basket and a greatcoat.* POZZO *a whip.*]

POZZO: [*Off.*] On! [*Crack of whip.* POZZO *appears. They cross the stage.* LUCKY *passes before* VLADIMIR *and* ESTRAGON *and exits.* POZZO *at the sight of* VLADIMIR *and* ESTRAGON *stops short. The rope tautens.* POZZO *jerks it violently.*] Back!
[*Noise of* LUCKY *falling with all his baggage.* VLADIMIR *and* ESTRAGON *turn towards him, half wishing, half fearing to go to his assistance.* VLADIMIR *takes a step towards* LUCKY, ESTRAGON *holds him back by the sleeve.*]

VLADIMIR: Let me go!

ESTRAGON: Stay where you are!

POZZO: Be careful! He's wicked. [VLADIMIR *and*
ESTRAGON *turn towards* POZZO.] With strangers.
ESTRAGON: [*Undertone.*] Is that him?
VLADIMIR: Who?
ESTRAGON: [*Trying to remember the name.*] Er . . .
VLADIMIR: Godot?
ESTRAGON: Yes.
POZZO: I present myself: Pozzo.
VLADIMIR: [*To* ESTRAGON.] Not at all!
ESTRAGON: He said Godot.
VLADIMIR: Not at all!
ESTRAGON: [*Timidly to* POZZO.] You're not Mr Godot, sir?
POZZO: [*Terrifying voice.*] I am Pozzo! [*Silence.*] Pozzo!
[*Silence.*] Does that name mean nothing to you?
[*Silence.*] I say does that name mean nothing to you?
[VLADIMIR *and* ESTRAGON *look at each other
questioningly.*]
ESTRAGON: [*Pretending to search.*] Bozzo . . . Bozzo . . .
VLADIMIR: [*Ditto.*] Pozzo . . . Pozzo . . .
POZZO: PPPOZZZZO!
ESTRAGON: Ah! Pozzo . . . let me see . . . Pozzo . . .
VLADIMIR: It is Pozzo or Bozzo?
ESTRAGON: Pozzo . . . no . . . I'm afraid I . . . no . . . I
don't seem to . . .
[POZZO *advances threateningly.*]
VLADIMIR: [*Conciliating.*] I once knew a family called
Gozzo. The mother had the clap.
ESTRAGON: [*Hastily.*] We're not from these parts, sir.
POZZO: [*Halting.*] You are human beings none the less.
[*He puts on his glasses.*] As far as one can see. [*He
takes off his glasses.*] Of the same species as myself.
[*He bursts into an enormous laugh.*] Of the same
species as Pozzo! Made in God's image!
VLADIMIR: Well you see –
POZZO: [*Peremptory.*] Who is Godot?
ESTRAGON: Godot?

POZZO: You took me for Godot.

ESTRAGON: Oh no, sir, not for an instant, sir.

POZZO: Who is he?

VLADIMIR: Oh, he's a . . . he's a kind of acquaintance.

ESTRAGON: Nothing of the kind, we hardly know him.

VLADIMIR: True . . . we don't know him very well . . . but all the same . . .

ESTRAGON: Personally I wouldn't even know him if I saw him.

POZZO: You took me for him.

ESTRAGON: [*Recoiling before* POZZO.] That's to say . . . you understand . . . the dusk . . . the strain . . . waiting . . . I confess . . . I imagined . . . for a second . . .

POZZO: Waiting? So you were waiting for him?

VLADIMIR: Well you see –

POZZO: Here? On my land?

VLADIMIR: We didn't intend any harm.

ESTRAGON: We meant well.

POZZO: The road is free to all.

VLADIMIR: That's how we looked at it.

POZZO: It's a disgrace. But there you are.

ESTRAGON: Nothing we can do about it.

POZZO: [*With magnanimous gesture.*] Let's say no more about it. [*He jerks the rope.*] Up pig! [*Pause.*] Every time he drops he falls asleep. [*Jerks the rope.*] Up hog! [*Noise of* LUCKY *getting up and picking up his baggage.* POZZO *jerks the rope.*] Back! [*Enter* LUCKY *backwards.*] Stop! [LUCKY *stops.*] Turn! [LUCKY *turns. To* VLADIMIR *and* ESTRAGON, *affably.*] Gentlemen, I am happy to have met you. [*Before their incredulous expression.*] Yes, yes, sincerely happy. [*He jerks the rope.*] Closer! [LUCKY *advances.*] Stop! [LUCKY *stops.*] Yes, the road seems long when one journeys all alone for . . . [*He consults his watch*] . . . yes . . . [*He calculates*] . . . yes, six hours, that's right, six hours on end, and never a soul in sight. [*To* LUCKY.]

Coat! [LUCKY *puts down the bag, advances, gives the coat, goes back to his place, takes up the bag.*] Hold that! [POZZO *holds out the whip.* LUCKY *advances and, both his hands being occupied, takes the whip in his mouth, then goes back to his place.* POZZO *begins to put on his coat, stops.*] Coat! [LUCKY *puts down bag, basket and stool, advances, helps* POZZO *on with his coat, goes back to his place and takes up bag, basket and stool.*] Touch of autumn in the air this evening. [POZZO *finishes buttoning his coat, stoops, inspects himself, straightens up.*] Whip! [LUCKY *advances, stoops,* POZZO *snatches the whip from his mouth,* LUCKY *goes back to his place.*] Yes, gentlemen, I cannot go for long without the society of my likes [*He puts on his glasses and looks at the two likes*] even when the likeness is an imperfect one. [*He takes off his glasses.*] Stool! [LUCKY *puts down bag and basket, advances, opens stool, puts it down, goes back to his place, takes up bag and basket.*] Closer! [LUCKY *puts down bag and basket, advances, moves stool, goes back to his place, takes up bag and basket.* POZZO *sits down, places the butt of his whip against* LUCKY'*s chest and pushes.*] Back! [LUCKY *takes a step back.*] Further! [LUCKY *takes another step back.*] Stop! [LUCKY *stops. To* VLADIMIR *and* ESTRAGON.] That is why, with your permission, I propose to dally with you a moment, before I venture any further. Basket! [LUCKY *advances, gives the basket, goes back to his place.*] The fresh air stimulates the jaded appetite. [*He opens the basket, takes out a piece of chicken and a bottle of wine.*] Basket! [LUCKY *advances, picks up the basket, goes back to his place.*] Further! [LUCKY *takes a step back.*] He stinks. Happy days! [*He drinks from the bottle, puts it down and begins to eat. Silence.* VLADIMIR *and* ESTRAGON, *cautiously at first, then more boldly, begin to circle about* LUCKY,

inspecting him up and down. POZZO *eats his chicken
voraciously, throwing away the bones after having
sucked them.* LUCKY *sags slowly, until bag and
basket touch the ground, then straightens up with a
start and begins to sag again. Rhythm of one sleeping
on his feet.*]

ESTRAGON: What ails him?

VLADIMIR: He looks tired.

ESTRAGON: Why doesn't he put down his bags?

VLADIMIR: How do I know? [*They close in on him.*]
Careful!

ESTRAGON: Say something to him.

VLADIMIR: Look!

ESTRAGON: What?

VLADIMIR: [*Pointing.*] His neck!

ESTRAGON: [*Looking at his neck.*] I see nothing.

VLADIMIR: Here.

[ESTRAGON *goes over beside* VLADIMIR.]

ESTRAGON: Oh I say.

VLADIMIR: A running sore!

ESTRAGON: It's the rope.

VLADIMIR: It's the rubbing.

ESTRAGON: It's inevitable.

VLADIMIR: It's the knot.

ESTRAGON: It's the chafing.

[*They resume their inspection, dwell on the face.*]

VLADIMIR: [*Grudgingly.*] He's not bad looking.

ESTRAGON: [*Shrugging his shoulders, wry face.*] Would
you say so?

VLADIMIR: A trifle effeminate.

ESTRAGON: Look at the slobber.

VLADIMIR: It's inevitable.

ESTRAGON: Look at the slaver.

VLADIMIR: Perhaps he's a half-wit.

ESTRAGON: A cretin.

VLADIMIR: [*Looking closer.*] It looks like a goitre.

ESTRAGON: [*Ditto.*] It's not certain.

VLADIMIR: He's panting.

ESTRAGON: It's inevitable.

VLADIMIR: And his eyes!

ESTRAGON: What about them?

VLADIMIR: Goggling out of his head.

ESTRAGON: Looks at his last gasp to me.

VLADIMIR: It's not certain. [*Pause.*] Ask him a question.

ESTRAGON: Would that be a good thing?

VLADIMIR: What do we risk?

ESTRAGON: [*Timidly.*] Mister . . .

VLADIMIR: Louder.

ESTRAGON: Mister . . .

POZZO: Leave him in peace! [*They turn towards* POZZO, *who, having finished eating, wipes his mouth with the back of his hand.*] Can't you see he wants to rest? Basket! [*He strikes a match and begins to light his pipe.* ESTRAGON *sees the chicken bones on the ground and stares at them greedily. As* LUCKY *does not move* POZZO *throws the match angrily away and jerks the rope.*] Basket! [LUCKY *starts, almost falls, recovers his senses, advances, puts the bottle in the basket, returns to his place.* ESTRAGON *stares at the bones.* POZZO *strikes another match and lights his pipe.*] What can you expect, it's not his job. [*He pulls at his pipe, stretches out his legs.*] Ah! That's better.

ESTRAGON: [*Timidly.*] Please, sir . . .

POZZO: What is it, my good man?

ESTRAGON: Er . . . you've finished with the . . . er . . . you don't need the . . . er . . . bones, sir?

VLADIMIR: [*Scandalized.*] You couldn't have waited?

POZZO: No no, he does well to ask. Do I need the bones? [*He turns them over with the end of his whip.*] No, personally I do not need them any more. [ESTRAGON *takes a step towards the bones.*] But . . . [ESTRAGON *stops short*] . . . but in theory the bones go to the carrier. He is therefore the one to ask. [ESTRAGON *turns towards* LUCKY, *hesitates.*] Go on, go on, don't be afraid, ask him, he'll tell you.] [ESTRAGON *goes towards* LUCKY, *stops before him.*]

ESTRAGON: Mister. . . excuse me, Mister. . .

POZZO: You're being spoken to, pig! Reply! [*To* ESTRAGON.] Try him again.

ESTRAGON: Excuse me, Mister, the bones, you won't be wanting the bones?

[LUCKY *looks long at* ESTRAGON.]

POZZO: [*In raptures.*] Mister! [LUCKY *bows his head.*] Reply! Do you want them or don't you? [*Silence of* LUCKY. *To* ESTRAGON.] They're yours. [ESTRAGON *makes a dart at the bones, picks them up and begins to gnaw them.*] I don't like it. I've never known him refuse a bone before. [*He looks anxiously at* LUCKY.] Nice business it'd be if he fell sick on me! [*He puffs at his pipe.*]

VLADIMIR: [*Exploding.*] It's a scandal!

[*Silence. Flabbergasted,* ESTRAGON *stops gnawing, looks at* POZZO *and* VLADIMIR *in turn.* POZZO *outwardly calm.* VLADIMIR *embarrassed.*]

POZZO: [*To* VLADIMIR.] Are you alluding to anything in particular?

VLADIMIR: [*Stutteringly resolute.*] To treat a man . . . [*Gesture towards* LUCKY] . . . like that . . . I think that . . . no . . . a human being . . . no . . . it's a scandal!

ESTRAGON: [*Not to be outdone.*] A disgrace! [*He resumes his gnawing.*]

POZZO: You are severe. [*To* VLADIMIR.] What age are you, if it's not a rude question. [*Silence.*] Sixty? Seventy? [*To* ESTRAGON.] What age would you say he was?

ESTRAGON: Eleven.

POZZO: I am impertinent. [*He knocks out his pipe against the whip, gets up.*] I must be getting on. Thank you for

your society. [*He reflects.*] Unless I smoke another pipe
before I go. What do you say? [*They say nothing.*] Oh,
I'm only a small smoker, a very small smoker, I'm not
in the habit of smoking two pipes one on top of the
other, it makes [*Hand to heart, sighing*] my heart go
pit-a-pat. [*Silence.*] It's the nicotine, one absorbs it in
spite of one's precautions. [*Sighs.*] You know how it is.
[*Silence.*] But perhaps you don't smoke? Yes? No? It's
of no importance. [*Silence.*] But how am I to sit down
now, without affectation, now that I have risen?
Without appearing to – how shall I say – without
appearing to falter. [*To* VLADIMIR.] I beg your
pardon? [*Silence.*] Perhaps you didn't speak? [*Silence.*]
It's of no importance. Let me see . . . [*He reflects.*]

ESTRAGON: Ah! That's better.

[*He puts the bones in his pocket.*]

VLADIMIR: Let's go.

ESTRAGON: So soon?

POZZO: One moment. [*He jerks the rope.*] Stool! [*He
points with his whip. Lucky moves the stool.*] More!
There! [*He sits down.* LUCKY *goes back to his place.*]
Done it! [*He fills his pipe.*]

VLADIMIR: [*Vehemently.*] Let's go!

POZZO: I hope I'm not driving you away. Wait a little
longer, you'll never regret it.

ESTRAGON: [*Scenting charity.*] We're in no hurry.

POZZO: [*Having lit his pipe.*] The second is never so
sweet . . . [*He takes the pipe out of his mouth,
contemplates it*] . . . as the first, I mean. [*He puts the
pipe back in his mouth.*] But it's sweet just the same.

VLADIMIR: I'm going.

POZZO: He can no longer endure my presence. I am
perhaps not particularly human, but who cares? [*To*
VLADIMIR.] Think twice before you do anything rash.
Suppose you go now, while it is still day, for there is
no denying it is still day. [*They all look up at the sky.*]

Good. [*They stop looking at the sky.*] What happens
in that case – [*He takes the pipe out of his mouth,
examines it*] – I'm out – [*He relights his pipe*] – in that
case – [*Puff*] – in that case – [*Puff*] – what happens in
that case to your appointment with this . . . Godet
. . . Godot . . . Godin . . . anyhow you see who I
mean, who has your future in his hands . . . [*Pause*]
. . . at least your immediate future.

VLADIMIR: Who told you?

POZZO: He speaks to me again! If this goes on much
longer we'll soon be old friends.

ESTRAGON: Why doesn't he put down his bags?

POZZO: I too would be happy to meet him. The more
people I meet the happier I become. From the meanest
creature one departs wiser, richer, more conscious of
one's blessings. Even you . . . [*He looks at them
ostentatiously in turn to make it clear they are both
meant*] . . . even you, who knows, will have added to
my store.

ESTRAGON: Why doesn't he put down his bags?

POZZO: But that would surprise me.

VLADIMIR: You're being asked a question.

POZZO: [*Delighted.*] A question! Who? What? A moment
ago you were calling me sir, in fear and trembling. Now
you're asking me questions. No good will come of this!

VLADIMIR: [*To* ESTRAGON.] I think he's listening.

ESTRAGON: [*Circling about* LUCKY.] What?

VLADIMIR: You can ask him now. He's on the alert.

ESTRAGON: Ask him what?

VLADIMIR: Why he doesn't put down his bags.

ESTRAGON: I wonder.

VLADIMIR: Ask him, can't you?

POZZO: [*Who has followed these exchanges with anxious
attention, fearing lest the question get lost.*] You want
to know why he doesn't put down his bags, as you
call them?

VLADIMIR: That's it.

POZZO: [*To* ESTRAGON.] You are sure you agree with that?

ESTRAGON: He's puffing like a grampus.

POZZO: The answer is this. [*To* ESTRAGON.] But stay still, I beg of you, you're making me nervous!

VLADIMIR: Here.

ESTRAGON: What is it?

VLADIMIR: He's about to speak.

[ESTRAGON *goes over beside* VLADIMIR. *Motionless, side by side, they wait.*]

POZZO: Good. Is everybody ready? Is everybody looking at me? [*He looks at* LUCKY, *jerks the rope.* LUCKY *raises his head.*] Will you look at me, pig! [LUCKY *looks at him.*] Good. [*He puts his pipe in his pocket, takes out a little vaporizer and sprays his throat, puts back the vaporizer in his pocket, clears his throat, spits, takes out the vaporizer again, sprays his throat again, puts back the vaporizer in his pocket.*] I am ready. Is everybody listening? Is everybody ready? [*He looks at them all in turn, jerks the rope.*] Hog! [LUCKY *raises his head.*] I don't like talking in a vacuum. Good. Let me see.
[*He reflects.*]

ESTRAGON: I'm going.

POZZO: What was it exactly you wanted to know?

VLADIMIR: Why he –

POZZO: [*Angrily.*] Don't interrupt me! [*Pause. Calmer.*] If we all speak at once we'll never get anywhere. [*Pause.*] What was I saying? [*Pause. Louder.*] What was I saying?
[VLADIMIR *mimics one carrying a heavy burden.* POZZO *looks at him, puzzled.*]

ESTRAGON: [*Forcibly.*] Bags. [*He points at* LUCKY.] Why? Always hold. [*He sags, panting.*] Never put down. [*He opens his hands, straightens up with relief.*] Why?

POZZO: Ah! Why couldn't you say so before? Why he
doesn't make himself comfortable? Let's try and get it
clear. Has he not the right to? Certainly he has. It
follows that he doesn't want to. There's reasoning for
you. And why doesn't he want to? [*Pause.*] Gentlemen,
the reason is this.

VLADIMIR: [*To* ESTRAGON.] Make a note of this.

POZZO: He wants to impress me, so that I'll keep him.

ESTRAGON: What?

POZZO: Perhaps I haven't got it quite right. He wants to
mollify me, so that I'll give up the idea of parting with
him. No, that's not exactly it either.

VLADIMIR: You want to get rid of him?

POZZO: He wants to cod me, but he won't.

VLADIMIR: You want to get rid of him?

POZZO: He imagines that when I see how well he carries
I'll be tempted to keep him on in that capacity.

ESTRAGON: You've had enough of him?

POZZO: In reality he carries like a pig. It's not his job.

VLADIMIR: You want to get rid of him?

POZZO: He imagines that when I see him indefatigable I'll
regret my decision. Such is his miserable scheme. As
though I were short of slaves! [*All three look at*
LUCKY.] Atlas, son of Jupiter! [*Silence.*] Well, that's
that, I think. Anything else? [*Vaporizer.*]

VLADIMIR: You want to get rid of him?

POZZO: Remark that I might just as well have been in his
shoes and he in mine. If chance had not willed
otherwise. To each one his due.

VLADIMIR: You waagerrim?

POZZO: I beg your pardon?

VLADIMIR: You want to get rid of him?

POZZO: I do. But instead of driving him away as I might
have done, I mean instead of simply kicking him out
on his arse, in the goodness of my heart I am bringing
him to the fair, where I hope to get a good price for

him. The truth is you can't drive such creatures away.
The best thing would be to kill them.

[LUCKY *weeps.*]

ESTRAGON: He's crying.

POZZO: Old dogs have more dignity. [*He proffers his
handkerchief to* ESTRAGON.] Comfort him, since you
pity him. [ESTRAGON *hesitates.*] Come on.
[ESTRAGON *takes the handkerchief.*] Wipe away his
tears, he'll feel less forsaken.
[ESTRAGON *hesitates.*]

VLADIMIR: Here, give it to me, I'll do it.
[ESTRAGON *refuses to give the handkerchief. Childish
gestures.*]

POZZO: Make haste, before he stops. [ESTRAGON
approaches LUCKY *and makes to wipe his eyes.* LUCKY
kicks him violently in the shins. ESTRAGON *drops the
handkerchief, recoils, staggers about the stage howling
with pain.*] Hanky!
[LUCKY *puts down bag and basket, picks up
handkerchief, gives it to* POZZO, *goes back to his
place, picks up bag and basket.*]

ESTRAGON: Oh the swine! [*He pulls up the leg of his
trousers.*] He's crippled me!

POZZO: I told you he didn't like strangers.

VLADIMIR: [*To* ESTRAGON.] Show. [ESTRAGON *shows
his leg. To* POZZO, *angrily.*] He's bleeding!

POZZO: It's a good sign.

ESTRAGON: [*On one leg.*] I'll never walk again!

VLADIMIR: [*Tenderly.*] I'll carry you. [*Pause.*] If necessary.

POZZO: He's stopped crying. [*To* ESTRAGON.] You have
replaced him as it were. [*Lyrically.*] The tears of the
world are a constant quantity. For each one who
begins to weep, somewhere else another stops. The
same is true of the laugh. [*He laughs.*] Let us not then
speak ill of our generation, it is not any unhappier
than its predecessors. [*Pause.*] Let us not speak well

of it either. [*Pause.*] Let us not speak of it at all.
[*Pause. Judiciously.*] It is true the population has
increased.

VLADIMIR: Try and walk.

[ESTRAGON *takes a few limping steps, stops before*
LUCKY *and spits on him, then goes and sits down on
the mound.*]

POZZO: Guess who taught me all these beautiful things.
[*Pause. Pointing to* LUCKY.] My Lucky!

VLADIMIR: [*Looking at the sky.*] Will night never come?

POZZO: But for him all my thoughts, all my feelings,
would have been of common things. [*Pause. With
extraordinary vehemence.*] Professional worries!
[*Calmer.*] Beauty, grace, truth of the first water, I
knew they were all beyond me. So I took a knook.

VLADIMIR: [*Startled from his inspection of the sky.*] A
knook?

POZZO: That was nearly sixty years ago . . . [*He consults
his watch*] . . . yes, nearly sixty. [*Drawing himself up
proudly.*] You wouldn't think it to look at me, would
you? Compared to him I look like a young man, no?
[*Pause.*] Hat! [LUCKY *puts down the basket and takes
off his hat. His long white hair falls about his face. He
puts his hat under his arm and picks up the basket.*]
Now look. [POZZO *takes off his hat.*[1] *He is completely
bald. He puts on his hat again.*] Did you see?

VLADIMIR: And now you turn him away? Such an old
and faithful servant.

ESTRAGON: Swine!

[POZZO *more and more agitated.*]

VLADIMIR: After having sucked all the good out of him
you chuck him away like a . . . like a banana skin.
Really . . .

POZZO: [*Groaning, clutching his head.*] I can't bear it . . .

---

[1] All four wear bowlers.

any longer . . . the way he goes on . . . you've no idea
. . . it's terrible . . . he must go . . . [*He waves his
arms*] . . . I'm going mad . . . [*He collapses, his head
in his hands*] . . . I can't bear it . . . any longer . . .
[*Silence. All look at* POZZO.]

VLADIMIR: He can't bear it.

ESTRAGON: Any longer.

VLADIMIR: He's going mad.

ESTRAGON: It's terrible.

VLADIMIR: [*To* LUCKY.] How dare you! It's abominable!
Such a good master! Crucify him like that! After so
many years! Really!

POZZO: [*Sobbing.*] He used to be so kind . . . so helpful
. . . and entertaining . . . my good angel . . . and now
. . . he's killing me.

ESTRAGON: [*To* VLADIMIR.] Does he want to replace him?

VLADIMIR: What?

ESTRAGON: Does he want someone to take his place or
not?

VLADIMIR: I don't think so.

ESTRAGON: What?

VLADIMIR: I don't know.

ESTRAGON: Ask him.

POZZO: [*Calmer.*] Gentlemen, I don't know what came
over me. Forgive me. Forget all I said. [*More and
more his old self.*] I don't remember exactly what it
was, but you may be sure there wasn't a word of
truth in it. [*Drawing himself up, striking his chest.*]
Do I look like a man that can be made to suffer?
Frankly? [*He rummages in his pockets.*] What have I
done with my pipe?

VLADIMIR: Charming evening we're having.

ESTRAGON: Unforgettable.

VLADIMIR: And it's not over.

ESTRAGON: Apparently not.

VLADIMIR: It's only beginning.

ESTRAGON: It's awful.

VLADIMIR: Worse than the pantomime.

ESTRAGON: The circus.

VLADIMIR: The music-hall.

ESTRAGON: The circus.

POZZO: What can I have done with that briar?

ESTRAGON: He's a scream. He's lost his dudeen.
  [*Laughs noisily.*]

VLADIMIR: I'll be back.
  [*He hastens towards the wings.*]

ESTRAGON: End of the corridor, on the left.

VLADIMIR: Keep my seat.
  [*Exit* VLADIMIR.]

POZZO: I've lost my Kapp and Peterson!

ESTRAGON: [*Convulsed with merriment.*] He'll be the
  death of me!

POZZO: [*Looking up.*] You didn't by any chance see – [*He
  misses* VLADIMIR.] Oh! He's gone! Without saying
  good-bye! How could he! He might have waited!

ESTRAGON: He would have burst.

POZZO: Oh! [*Pause.*] Oh well then of course in that case . . .

ESTRAGON: Come here.

POZZO: What for?

ESTRAGON: You'll see.

POZZO: You want me to get up?

ESTRAGON: Quick! [POZZO *gets up and goes over beside*
  ESTRAGON. ESTRAGON *points off.*] Look!

POZZO: [*Having put on his glasses.*] Oh I say!

ESTRAGON: It's all over.
  [*Enter* VLADIMIR, *sombre. He shoulders* LUCKY *out
  of his way, kicks over the stool, comes and goes
  agitatedly.*]

POZZO: He's not pleased.

ESTRAGON: [*To* VLADIMIR.] You missed a treat. Pity.
  [VLADIMIR *halts, straightens the stool, comes and
  goes, calmer.*]

POZZO: He subsides. [*Looking around.*] Indeed all
subsides. A great calm descends. [*Raising his hand.*]
Listen! Pan sleeps.

VLADIMIR: Will night never come?
[*All three look at the sky.*]

POZZO: You don't feel like going until it does?

ESTRAGON: Well you see –

POZZO: Why it's very natural, very natural. I myself in
your situation, if I had an appointment with a Godin
. . . Godet . . . Godot . . . anyhow, you see who I
mean, I'd wait till it was black night before I gave up.
[*He looks at the stool.*] I'd like very much to sit down,
but I don't quite know how to go about it.

ESTRAGON: Could I be of any help?

POZZO: If you asked me perhaps.

ESTRAGON: What?

POZZO: If you asked me to sit down.

ESTRAGON: Would that be a help?

POZZO: I fancy so.

ESTRAGON: Here we go. Be seated, sir, I beg of you.

POZZO: No, no, I wouldn't think of it! [*Pause. Aside.*]
Ask me again.

ESTRAGON: Come come, take a seat, I beseech you, you'll
get pneumonia.

POZZO: You really think so?

ESTRAGON: Why it's absolutely certain.

POZZO: No doubt you are right. [*He sits down.*] Done it
again! [*Pause.*] Thank you, dear fellow. [*He consults
his watch.*] But I must really be getting along, if I am
to observe my schedule.

VLADIMIR: Time has stopped.

POZZO: [*Cuddling his watch to his ear.*] Don't you
believe it, sir, don't you believe it. [*He puts his watch
back in his pocket.*] Whatever you like, but not that.

ESTRAGON: [*To* POZZO.] Everything seems black to him
today.

POZZO: Except the firmament! [*He laughs, pleased with this witticism.*] But I see what it is, you are not from these parts, you don't know what our twilights can do. Shall I tell you? [*Silence.* ESTRAGON *is fiddling with his boot again,* VLADIMIR *with his hat.*] I can't refuse you. [*Vaporizer.*] A little attention, if you please. [VLADIMIR *and* ESTRAGON *continue their fiddling,* LUCKY *is half asleep.* POZZO *cracks his whip feebly.*] What's the matter with this whip? [*He gets up and cracks it more vigorously, finally with success.* LUCKY *jumps.* VLADIMIR'*s hat,* ESTRAGON'*s boot,* LUCKY'*s hat, fall to the ground.* POZZO *throws down the whip.*] Worn out, this whip. [*He looks at* VLADIMIR *and* ESTRAGON.] What was I saying?

VLADIMIR: Let's go.

ESTRAGON: But take the weight off your feet, I implore you, you'll catch your death.

POZZO: True. [*He sits down. To* ESTRAGON.] What is your name?

ESTRAGON: Adam.

POZZO: [*Who hasn't listened.*] Ah, yes! The night. [*He raises his head.*] But be a little more attentive, for pity's sake, otherwise we'll never get anywhere. [*He looks at the sky.*] Look. [*All look at the sky except* LUCKY, *who is dozing off again.* POZZO *jerks the rope.*] Will you look at the sky, pig! [LUCKY *looks at the sky.*] Good, that's enough. [*They stop looking at the sky.*] What is there so extraordinary about it? Qua sky. It is pale and luminous like any sky at this hour of the day. [*Pause.*] In these latitudes. [*Pause.*] When the weather is fine. [*Lyrical.*] An hour ago [*He looks at his watch, prosaic*] roughly [*Lyrical*] after having poured forth ever since [*He hesitates, prosaic*] say ten o'clock in the morning [*Lyrical*] tirelessly torrents of red and white light it begins to lose its effulgence, to grow pale [*Gestures of the two hands lapsing by*

34

stages], pale, ever a little paler, a little paler until [*Dramatic pause, ample gesture of the two hands flung wide apart*] pppfff! finished! it comes to rest. But – [*Hand raised in admonition*] – but behind this veil of gentleness and peace night is charging [*Vibrantly*] and will burst upon us [*Snaps his fingers*] pop! like that! [*His inspiration leaves him*] just when we least expect it. [*Silence. Gloomily.*] That's how it is on this bitch of an earth.

[*Long silence.*]

ESTRAGON: So long as one knows.

VLADIMIR: One can bide one's time.

ESTRAGON: One knows what to expect.

VLADIMIR: No further need to worry.

ESTRAGON: Simply wait.

VLADIMIR: We're used to it.

[*He picks up his hat, looks inside it, shakes it, puts it on.*]

POZZO: How did you find me? [VLADIMIR *and* ESTRAGON *look at him blankly.*] Good? Fair? Middling? Poor? Positively bad?

VLADIMIR: [*First to understand.*] Oh very good, very very good.

POZZO: [*To* ESTRAGON.] And you, sir?

ESTRAGON: Oh, tray bong, tray tray tray bong.

POZZO: [*Fervently.*] Bless you, gentlemen, bless you! [*Pause.*] I have such need of encouragement! [*Pause.*] I weakened a little towards the end, you didn't notice?

VLADIMIR: Oh, perhaps just a teeny weeny little bit.

ESTRAGON: I thought it was intentional.

POZZO: You see my memory is defective.

[*Silence.*]

ESTRAGON: In the meantime nothing happens.

POZZO: You find it tedious?

ESTRAGON: Somewhat.

POZZO: [*To* VLADIMIR.] And you, sir?

VLADIMIR: I've been better entertained.

[*Silence.* POZZO *struggles inwardly.*]

POZZO: Gentlemen, you have been . . . civil to me.

ESTRAGON: Not at all.

VLADIMIR: What an idea!

POZZO: Yes yes, you have been correct. So that I ask myself is there anything I can do in my turn for these honest fellows who are having such a dull, dull time.

ESTRAGON: Even ten francs would be welcome.

VLADIMIR: We are not beggars!

POZZO: Is there anything I can do, that's what I ask myself, to cheer them up? I have given them bones, I have talked to them about this and that, I have explained the twilight, admittedly. But is it enough, that's what tortures me, is it enough?

ESTRAGON: Even five.

VLADIMIR: [*To* ESTRAGON, *indignantly.*] That's enough!

ESTRAGON: I couldn't accept less.

POZZO: Is it enough? No doubt. But I am liberal. It's my nature. This evening. So much the worse for me. [*He jerks the rope.* LUCKY *looks at him.*] For I shall suffer, no doubt about that. [*He picks up the whip.*] What do you prefer? Shall we have him dance, or sing, or recite, or think, or –

ESTRAGON: Who?

POZZO: Who! You know how to think, you two?

VLADIMIR: He thinks?

POZZO: Certainly. Aloud. He even used to think very prettily once, I could listen to him for hours. Now . . . [*He shudders.*] So much the worse for me. Well, would you like him to think something for us?

ESTRAGON: I'd rather he'd dance, it'd be more fun.

POZZO: Not necessarily.

ESTRAGON: Wouldn't it, Didi, be more fun?

VLADIMIR: I'd like well to hear him think.

ESTRAGON: Perhaps he could dance first and think
afterwards, if it isn't too much to ask him.

VLADIMIR: [*To* POZZO.] Would that be possible?

POZZO: By all means, nothing simpler. It's the natural order.
[*He laughs briefly.*]

VLADIMIR: Then let him dance.
[*Silence.*]

POZZO: Do you hear, hog?

ESTRAGON: He never refuses?

POZZO: He refused once. [*Silence.*] Dance, misery! [LUCKY
puts down the basket, advances towards front, turns to
POZZO. LUCKY *dances. He stops.*]

ESTRAGON: Is that all?

POZZO: Encore!
[LUCKY *executes the same movements, stops.*]

ESTRAGON: Pooh! I'd do as well myself. [*He imitates*
LUCKY, *almost falls.*] With a little practice.

POZZO: He used to dance the farandole, the fling, the
brawl, the jig, the fandango, and even the hornpipe.
He capered. For joy. Now that's the best he can do.
Do you know what he calls it?

ESTRAGON: The Scapegoat's Agony.

VLADIMIR: The Hard Stool.

POZZO: The Net. He thinks he's entangled in a net.

VLADIMIR: [*Squirming like an aesthete.*] There's
something about it . . .
[LUCKY *makes to return to his burdens.*]

POZZO: Woaa!
[LUCKY *stiffens.*]

ESTRAGON: Tell us about the time he refused.

POZZO: With pleasure, with pleasure. [*He fumbles in his
pockets.*] Wait. [*He fumbles.*] What have I done with
my spray? [*He fumbles.*] Well now isn't that . . . [*He
looks up, consternation on his features. Faintly.*] I
can't find my pulverizer!

ESTRAGON: [*Faintly.*] My left lung is very weak! [*He*

37

coughs feebly. In ringing tones.] But my right lung is as sound as a bell!

POZZO: [*Normal voice.*] No matter! What was I saying. [*He ponders.*] Wait. [*Ponders.*] Well now isn't that . . . [*He raises his head*]. Help me!

ESTRAGON: Wait!

VLADIMIR: Wait!

POZZO: Wait!

[*All three take off their hats simultaneously, press their hands to their foreheads, concentrate.*]

ESTRAGON: [*Triumphantly.*] Ah!

VLADIMIR: He has it.

POZZO: [*Impatient.*] Well?

ESTRAGON: Why doesn't he put down his bags?

VLADIMIR: Rubbish!

POZZO: Are you sure?

VLADIMIR: Damn it, haven't you already told us!

POZZO: I've already told you?

ESTRAGON: He's already told us?

VLADIMIR: Anyway he has put them down.

ESTRAGON: [*Glance at* LUCKY.] So he has. And what of it?

VLADIMIR: Since he has put down his bags it is impossible we should have asked why he does not do so.

POZZO: Stoutly reasoned!

ESTRAGON: And why has he put them down?

POZZO: Answer us that.

VLADIMIR: In order to dance.

ESTRAGON: True!

POZZO: True!

[*Silence. They put on their hats.*]

ESTRAGON: Nothing happens, nobody comes, nobody goes, it's awful!

VLADIMIR: [*To* POZZO.] Tell him to think.

POZZO: Give him his hat.

VLADIMIR: His hat?

POZZO: He can't think without his hat.
VLADIMIR: [*To* ESTRAGON.] Give him his hat.
ESTRAGON: Me! After what he did to me! Never!
VLADIMIR: I'll give it to him.
    [*He does not move.*]
ESTRAGON: [*To* POZZO.] Tell him to go and fetch it.
POZZO: It's better to give it to him.
VLADIMIR: I'll give it to him.
    [*He picks up the hat and tenders it at arm's length to*
    LUCKY, *who does not move.*]
POZZO: You must put it on his head.
ESTRAGON: [*To* POZZO.] Tell him to take it.
POZZO: It's better to put it on his head.
VLADIMIR: I'll put it on his head.
    [*He goes round behind* LUCKY, *approaches him
    cautiously, puts the hat on his head and recoils
    smartly.* LUCKY *does not move. Silence.*]
ESTRAGON: What's he waiting for?
POZZO: Stand back! [VLADIMIR *and* ESTRAGON *move
    away from* LUCKY. POZZO *jerks the rope.* LUCKY
    looks at POZZO.] Think, pig! [*Pause.* LUCKY *begins
    to dance.*] Stop! [LUCKY *stops.*] Forward! [LUCKY
    advances.] Stop! [LUCKY *stops.*] Think!
    [*Silence.*]
LUCKY: On the other hand with regard to –
POZZO: Stop! [LUCKY *stops.*] Back! [LUCKY *moves back.*]
    Stop! [LUCKY *stops.*] Turn! [LUCKY *turns towards
    auditorium.*] Think!
    [*During* LUCKY's *tirade the others react as follows:
    [1]* VLADIMIR *and* ESTRAGON *all attention,* POZZO
    dejected and disgusted. [2] VLADIMIR *and*
    ESTRAGON *begin to protest,* POZZO's *sufferings
    increase. [3]* VLADIMIR *and* ESTRAGON *attentive
    again,* POZZO *more and more agitated and groaning.
    [4]* VLADIMIR *and* ESTRAGON *protest violently.*
    POZZO *jumps up, pulls on the rope. General outcry.*

LUCKY *pulls on the rope, staggers, shouts his text. All three throw themselves on* LUCKY *who struggles and shouts his text.*]

LUCKY: Given the existence as uttered forth in the public works of Puncher and Wattmann of a personal God quaquaquaqua with white beard quaquaquaqua outside time without extension who from the heights of divine apathia divine athambia divine aphasia loves us dearly with some exceptions for reasons unknown but time will tell and suffers like the divine Miranda with those who for reasons unknown but time will tell are plunged in torment plunged in fire whose fire flames if that continues and who can doubt it will fire the firmament that is to say blast hell to heaven so blue still and calm so calm with a calm which even though intermittent is better than nothing but not so fast and considering what is more that as a result of the labours left unfinished crowned by the Acacacacademy of Anthropopopometry of Essy-in-Possy of Testew and Cunard it is established beyond all doubt all other doubt than that which clings to the labours of men that as a result of the labours unfinished of Testew and Cunard it is established as hereinafter but not so fast for reasons unknown that as a result of the public works of Puncher and Wattmann it is established beyond all doubt that in view of the labours of Fartov and Belcher left unfinished for reasons unknown of Testew and Cunard left unfinished it is established what many deny that man in Possy of Testew and Cunard that man in Essy that man in short that man in brief in spite of the strides of alimentation and defecation is seen to waste and pine waste and pine and concurrently simultaneously what is more for reasons unknown in spite of the strides of physical culture the practice of sports such as tennis football running

cycling swimming flying floating riding gliding
conating camogie skating tennis of all kinds dying
flying sports of all sorts autumn summer winter
winter tennis of all kinds hockey of all sorts penicillin
and succedanea in a word I resume and concurrently
simultaneously for reasons unknown to shrink and
dwindle in spite of the tennis I resume flying gliding
golf over nine and eighteen holes tennis of all sorts in
a word for reasons unknown in Feckham Peckham
Fulham Clapham namely concurrently simultaneously
what is more for reasons unknown but time will tell
to shrink and dwindle I resume Fulham Clapham in a
word the dead loss per caput since the death of
Bishop Berkeley being to the tune of one inch four
ounce per caput approximately by and large more or
less to the nearest decimal good measure round
figures stark naked in the stockinged feet in
Connemara in a word for reasons unknown no
matter what matter the facts are there and considering
what is more much more grave that in the light of the
labours lost of Steinweg and Peterman it appears
what is more much more grave that in the light the
light the light of the labours lost of Steinweg and
Peterman that in the plains in the mountains by the
seas by the rivers running water running fire the air
is the same and then the earth namely the air and then
the earth in the great cold the great dark the air and
the earth abode of stones in the great cold alas alas
in the year of their Lord six hundred and something
the air the earth the sea the earth abode of stones
in the great deeps the great cold on sea on land and in
the air I resume for reasons unknown in spite of the
tennis the facts are there but time will tell I resume
alas alas on on in short in fine on on abode of stones
who can doubt it I resume but not so fast I resume the
skull to shrink and waste and concurrently

simultaneously what is more for reasons unknown in spite of the tennis on on the beard the flames the tears the stones so blue so calm alas alas on on the skull the skull the skull the skull in Connemara in spite of the tennis the labours abandoned left unfinished graver still abode of stones in a word I resume alas alas abandoned unfinished the skull the skull in Connemara in spite of the tennis the skull alas the stones Cunard [*Mêlée, final vociferations*] tennis . . . the stones . . . so calm . . . Cunard . . . unfinished . . .

POZZO: His hat!

[VLADIMIR *seizes* LUCKY'*s hat. Silence of* LUCKY. *He falls. Silence. Panting of the victors.*]

ESTRAGON: Avenged!

[VLADIMIR *examines the hat, peers inside it.*]

POZZO: Give me that! [*He snatches the hat from* VLADIMIR, *throws it on the ground, tramples on it.*] There's an end to his thinking!

VLADIMIR: But will he able to walk?

POZZO: Walk or crawl! [*He kicks* LUCKY.] Up pig!

ESTRAGON: Perhaps he's dead.

VLADIMIR: You'll kill him.

POZZO: Up scum! [*He jerks the rope.*] Help me!

VLADIMIR: How?

POZZO: Raise him up!

[VLADIMIR *and* ESTRAGON *hoist* LUCKY *to his feet, support him an instant, then let him go. He falls.*]

ESTRAGON: He's doing it on purpose!

POZZO: You must hold him. [*Pause.*] Come on, come on, raise him up!

ESTRAGON: To hell with him!

VLADIMIR: Come on, once more.

ESTRAGON: What does he take us for?

[*They raise* LUCKY, *hold him up.*]

POZZO: Don't let him go! [VLADIMIR *and* ESTRAGON *totter.*] Don't move! [POZZO *fetches bag and basket*

and brings them towards LUCKY.] Hold him tight!
[*He puts the bag in* LUCKY's *hand.* LUCKY *drops it
immediately.*] Don't let him go! [*He puts back the bag
in* LUCKY's *hand. Gradually, at the feel of the bag,*
LUCKY *recovers his senses and his fingers close round
the handle.*] Hold him tight! [*As before with basket.*]
Now! You can let him go. [VLADIMIR *and*
ESTRAGON *move away from* LUCKY, *who totters,
reels, sags, but succeeds in remaining on his feet, bag
and basket in his hands.* POZZO *steps back, cracks his
whip.*] Forward! [LUCKY *totters forward.*] Back!
[LUCKY *totters back.*] Turn! [LUCKY *turns.*] Done it!
He can walk. [*Turning towards* VLADIMIR *and*
ESTRAGON.] Thank you gentlemen, and let me . . .
[*He fumbles in his pockets*] . . . let me wish you . . .
[*Fumbles*] . . . wish you . . . [*Fumbles*] . . . what have
I done with my watch? [*Fumbles.*] A genuine half-
hunter, gentlemen, with deadbeat escapement!
[*Sobbing.*] 'Twas my granpa gave it to me!
[*He searches on the ground,* VLADIMIR *and* ESTRAGON
likewise. POZZO *turns over with his foot the remains of*
LUCKY's *hat.*] Well now, isn't that just –
VLADIMIR: Perhaps it's in your fob.
POZZO: Wait! [*He doubles up in an attempt to apply his
ear to his stomach, listens. Silence.*] I hear nothing.
[*He beckons them to approach.* VLADIMIR *and*
ESTRAGON *go towards him, bend over his stomach.*]
Surely one should hear the tick-tick.
VLADIMIR: Silence!
[*All listen, bent double.*]
ESTRAGON: I hear something.
POZZO: Where?
VLADIMIR: It's the heart.
POZZO: [*Disappointed.*] Damnation!
VLADIMIR: Silence!
ESTRAGON: Perhaps it has stopped.

[*They straighten up.*]

POZZO: Which of you smells so bad?

ESTRAGON: He has stinking breath and I have stinking feet.

POZZO: I must go.

ESTRAGON: And your half-hunter?

POZZO: I must have left it at the manor.

[*Silence.*]

ESTRAGON: Then adieu.

POZZO: Adieu.

VLADIMIR: Adieu.

POZZO: Adieu.

[*Silence. No one moves.*]

VLADIMIR: Adieu.

POZZO: Adieu.

ESTRAGON: Adieu.

[*Silence.*]

POZZO: And thank you.

VLADIMIR: Thank *you*.

POZZO: Not at all.

ESTRAGON: Yes yes.

POZZO: No no.

VLADIMIR: Yes yes.

ESTRAGON: No no.

[*Silence.*]

POZZO: I don't seem to be able . . . [*Long hesitation*] . . . to depart.

ESTRAGON: Such is life.

[POZZO *turns, moves away from* LUCKY *towards the wings, paying out the rope as he goes.*]

VLADIMIR: You're going the wrong way.

POZZO: I need a running start. [*Having come to the end of the rope, i.e. off stage, he stops, turns, and cries.*] Stand back! [VLADIMIR *and* ESTRAGON *stand back, look towards* POZZO. *Crack of whip.*] On! On!

ESTRAGON: On!

VLADIMIR: On!

[LUCKY *moves off.*]

POZZO: Faster!

[*He appears, crosses the stage preceded by* LUCKY. VLADIMIR *and* ESTRAGON *wave their hats. Exit* LUCKY.] On! On! [*On the point of disappearing in his turn he stops and turns. The rope tautens. Noise of* LUCKY *falling off.*] Stool! [VLADIMIR *fetches stool and gives it to* POZZO, *who throws it to* LUCKY.] Adieu.

VLADIMIR: ⎫
ESTRAGON: ⎭ [*Waving.*] Adieu! Adieu!

POZZO: Up! Pig! [*Noise of* LUCKY *getting up.*] On! [*Exit* POZZO.] Faster! On! Adieu! Pig! Yip! Adieu!

[*Long silence.*]

VLADIMIR: That passed the time.

ESTRAGON: It would have passed in any case.

VLADIMIR: Yes, but not so rapidly.

[*Pause.*]

ESTRAGON: What do we do now?

VLADIMIR: I don't know.

ESTRAGON: Let's go.

VLADIMIR: We can't.

ESTRAGON: Why not?

VLADIMIR: We're waiting for Godot.

ESTRAGON: [*Despairingly.*] Ah!

[*Pause.*]

VLADIMIR: How they've changed!

ESTRAGON: Who?

VLADIMIR: Those two.

ESTRAGON: That's the idea, let's make a little conversation.

VLADIMIR: Haven't they?

ESTRAGON: What?

VLADIMIR: Changed.

ESTRAGON: Very likely. They all change. Only we can't.

VLADIMIR: Likely! It's certain. Didn't you see them?

ESTRAGON: I suppose I did. But I don't know them.

VLADIMIR: Yes you do know them.

ESTRAGON: No I don't know them.

VLADIMIR: We know them, I tell you. You forget everything. [*Pause. To himself.*] Unless they're not the same . . .

ESTRAGON: Why didn't they recognize us then?

VLADIMIR: That means nothing. I too pretended not to recognize them. And then nobody ever recognizes us.

ESTRAGON: Forget it. What we need – Ow! [VLADIMIR *does not react.*] Ow!

VLADIMIR: [*To himself.*] Unless they're not the same . . .

ESTRAGON: Didi! It's the other foot!

[*He goes hobbling towards the mound.*]

VLADIMIR: Unless they're not the same . . .

BOY: [*Off.*] Mister!

[ESTRAGON *halts. Both look towards the voice.*]

ESTRAGON: Off we go again.

VLADIMIR: Approach, my child.

[*Enter* BOY, *timidly. He halts.*]

BOY: Mister Albert . . . ?

VLADIMIR: Yes.

ESTRAGON: What do you want?

VLADIMIR: Approach.

[*The* BOY *does not move.*]

ESTRAGON: [*Forcibly.*] Approach when you're told, can't you?

[*The* BOY *advances timidly, halts.*]

VLADIMIR: What is it?

BOY: Mr Godot . . .

VLADIMIR: Obviously . . . [*Pause.*] Approach.

ESTRAGON: [*Violently.*] Will you approach! [*The* BOY *advances timidly.*] What kept you so late?

VLADIMIR: You have a message from Mr Godot?

BOY: Yes, sir.

VLADIMIR: Well, what is it?

ESTRAGON: What kept you so late?
[*The* BOY *looks at them in turn, not knowing to which he should reply.*]
VLADIMIR: [*To* ESTRAGON.] Let him alone.
ESTRAGON: [*Violently.*] You let me alone! [*Advancing, to the* BOY.] Do you know what time it is?
BOY: [*Recoiling.*] It's not my fault, sir.
ESTRAGON: And whose is it? Mine?
BOY: I was afraid, sir.
ESTRAGON: Afraid of what? Of us? [*Pause.*] Answer me!
VLADIMIR: I know what it is, he was afraid of the others.
ESTRAGON: How long have you been here?
BOY: A good while, sir.
VLADIMIR: You were afraid of the whip.
BOY: Yes, sir.
VLADIMIR: The roars.
BOY: Yes, sir.
VLADIMIR: The two big men.
BOY: Yes, sir.
VLADIMIR: Do you know them?
BOY: No, sir.
VLADIMIR: Are you a native of these parts? [*Silence.*] Do you belong to these parts?
BOY: Yes, sir.
ESTRAGON: That's all a pack of lies. [*Shaking the* BOY *by the arm.*] Tell us the truth.
BOY: [*Trembling.*] But it is the truth, sir!
VLADIMIR: Will you let him alone! What's the matter with you? [ESTRAGON *releases the* BOY, *moves away, covering his face with his hands.* VLADIMIR *and the* BOY *observe him.* ESTRAGON *drops his hands. His face is convulsed.*] What's the matter with you?
ESTRAGON: I'm unhappy.
VLADIMIR: Not really! Since when?
ESTRAGON: I'd forgotten.
VLADIMIR: Extraordinary the tricks that memory plays!

47

[ESTRAGON *tries to speak, renounces, limps to his place, sits down and begins to take off his boots. To* BOY.] Well?

BOY: Mr Godot –

VLADIMIR: I've seen you before, haven't I?

BOY: I don't know, sir.

VLADIMIR: You don't know me?

BOY: No, sir.

VLADIMIR: It wasn't you came yesterday?

BOY: No, sir.

VLADIMIR: This is your first time?

BOY: Yes, sir.

[*Silence.*]

VLADIMIR: Words, words. [*Pause.*] Speak.

BOY: [*In a rush.*] Mr Godot told me to tell you he won't come this evening but surely tomorrow.

[*Silence.*]

VLADIMIR: Is that all?

BOY: Yes, sir.

[*Silence.*]

VLADIMIR: You work for Mr Godot?

BOY: Yes, sir.

VLADIMIR: What do you do?

BOY: I mind the goats, sir.

VLADIMIR: Is he good to you?

BOY: Yes, sir.

VLADIMIR: He doesn't beat you?

BOY: No, sir, not me.

VLADIMIR: Whom does he beat?

BOY: He beats my brother, sir.

VLADIMIR: Ah, you have a brother?

BOY: Yes, sir.

VLADIMIR: What does he do?

BOY: He minds the sheep, sir.

VLADIMIR: And why doesn't he beat you?

BOY: I don't know, sir.

VLADIMIR: He must be fond of you.

BOY: I don't know, sir.

[*Silence.*]

VLADIMIR: Does he give you enough to eat? [*The* BOY *hesitates.*] Does he feed you well?

BOY: Fairly well, sir.

VLADIMIR: You're not unhappy? [*The* BOY *hesitates.*] Do you hear me?

BOY: Yes, sir.

VLADIMIR: Well?

BOY: I don't know, sir.

VLADIMIR: You don't know if you're unhappy or not?

BOY: No, sir.

VLADIMIR: You're as bad as myself. [*Silence.*] Where do you sleep?

BOY: In the loft, sir.

VLADIMIR: With your brother?

BOY: Yes, sir.

VLADIMIR: In the hay?

BOY: Yes, sir.

[*Silence.*]

VLADIMIR: All right, you may go.

BOY: What am I to say to Mr Godot, sir?

VLADIMIR: Tell him . . . [*He hesitates*] . . . tell him you saw us. [*Pause.*] You did see us, didn't you?

BOY: Yes, sir.

[*He steps back, hesitates, turns and exit running. The light suddenly fails. In a moment it is night. The moon rises at back, mounts in the sky, stands still, shedding a pale light on the scene.*]

VLADIMIR: At last! [ESTRAGON *gets up and goes towards* VLADIMIR, *a boot in each hand. He puts them down at the edge of stage, straightens and contemplates the moon.*] What are you doing?

ESTRAGON: Pale for weariness.

VLADIMIR: Eh?

ESTRAGON: Of climbing heaven and gazing on the likes of us.

VLADIMIR: Your boots. What are you doing with your boots?

ESTRAGON: [*Turning to look at the boots.*] I'm leaving them there. [*Pause.*] Another will come, just as . . . as . . . as me, but with smaller feet, and they'll make him happy.

VLADIMIR: But you can't go barefoot!

ESTRAGON: Christ did.

VLADIMIR: Christ! What's Christ got to do with it? You're not going to compare yourself to Christ!

ESTRAGON: All my life I've compared myself to him.

VLADIMIR: But where he lived it was warm, it was dry!

ESTRAGON: Yes. And they crucified quick.
[*Silence.*]

VLADIMIR: We've nothing more to do here.

ESTRAGON: Nor anywhere else.

VLADIMIR: Ah Gogo, don't go on like that. Tomorrow everything will be better.

ESTRAGON: How do you make that out?

VLADIMIR: Did you not hear what the child said?

ESTRAGON: No.

VLADIMIR: He said that Godot was sure to come tomorrow. [*Pause.*] What do you say to that?

ESTRAGON: Then all we have to do is to wait on here.

VLADIMIR: Are you mad? We must take cover. [*He takes* ESTRAGON *by the arm.*] Come on.
[*He draws* ESTRAGON *after him.* ESTRAGON *yields, then resists. They halt.*]

ESTRAGON: [*Looking at the tree.*] Pity we haven't got a bit of rope.

VLADIMIR: Come on. It's cold.
[*He draws* ESTRAGON *after him. As before.*]

ESTRAGON: Remind me to bring a bit of rope tomorrow.

VLADIMIR: Yes. Come on.

[*He draws him after him. As before.*]

ESTRAGON: How long have we been together all the time now?

VLADIMIR: I don't know. Fifty years perhaps.

ESTRAGON: Do you remember the day I threw myself into the Rhône?

VLADIMIR: We were grape-harvesting.

ESTRAGON: You fished me out.

VLADIMIR: That's all dead and buried.

ESTRAGON: My clothes dried in the sun.

VLADIMIR: There's no good harking back on that. Come on.

[*He draws him after him. As before.*]

ESTRAGON: Wait.

VLADIMIR: I'm cold!

ESTRAGON: Wait! [*He moves away from* VLADIMIR.] I wonder if we wouldn't have been better off alone, each one for himself. [*He crosses the stage and sits down on the mound.*] We weren't made for the same road.

VLADIMIR: [*Without anger.*] It's not certain.

ESTRAGON: No, nothing is certain.

[VLADIMIR *slowly crosses the stage and sits down beside* ESTRAGON.]

VLADIMIR: We can still part, if you think it would be better.

ESTRAGON: It's not worth while now.

[*Silence.*]

VLADIMIR: No, it's not worth while now.

[*Silence.*]

ESTRAGON: Well, shall we go?

VLADIMIR: Yes, let's go.

[*They do not move.*]

CURTAIN

Act Two

Next day. Same time. Same place

ESTRAGON's *boots front centre, heels together, toes splayed.* LUCKY's *hat at same place.*
The tree has four or five leaves.
Enter VLADIMIR *agitatedly. He halts and looks long at the tree, then suddenly begins to move feverishly about the stage. He halts before the boots, picks one up, examines it, sniffs it, manifests disgust, puts it back carefully. Comes and goes. Halts extreme right and gazes into distance off, shading his eyes with his hand. Comes and goes. Halts extreme left, as before. Comes and goes. Halts suddenly and begins to sing loudly.*

VLADIMIR: A dog came in –
[*Having begun too high he stops, clears his throat, resumes.*]

A dog came in the kitchen
And stole a crust of bread.
Then cook up with a ladle
And beat him till he was dead.

Then all the dogs came running
And dug the dog a tomb –
[*He stops, broods, resumes.*]

Then all the dogs came running
And dug the dog a tomb
And wrote upon the tombstone
For the eyes of dogs to come:

A dog came in the kitchen
And stole a crust of bread.

Then cook up with a ladle
And beat him till he was dead.

Then all the dogs came running
And dug the dog a tomb –
[*He stops, broods, resumes.*]

Then all the dogs came running
And dug the dog a tomb –
[*He stops, broods. Softly.*]

And dug the dog a tomb . . .

[*He remains a moment silent and motionless, then begins to move feverishly about the stage. He halts before the tree, comes and goes, before the boots, comes and goes, halts extreme right, gazes into distance, extreme left, gazes into distance. Enter* ESTRAGON *right, barefoot, head bowed. He slowly crosses the stage.* VLADIMIR *turns and sees him.*] You again! [ESTRAGON *halts, but does not raise his head.* VLADIMIR *goes towards him.*] Come here till I embrace you.

ESTRAGON: Don't touch me!
[VLADIMIR *holds back, pained.*]

VLADIMIR: Do you want me to go away? [*Pause.*] Gogo! [*Pause.* VLADIMIR *observes him attentively.*] Did they beat you? [*Pause.*] Gogo! [ESTRAGON *remains silent, head bowed.*] Where did you spend the night?

ESTRAGON: Don't touch me! Don't question me! Don't speak to me! Stay with me!

VLADIMIR: Did I ever leave you?

ESTRAGON: You let me go.

VLADIMIR: Look at me. [ESTRAGON *does not raise his head. Violently.*] Will you look at me!
[ESTRAGON *raises his head. They look long at each other, then suddenly embrace, clapping each other on*

the back. End of the embrace. ESTRAGON, *no longer supported, almost falls.*]

ESTRAGON: What a day!

VLADIMIR: Who beat you? Tell me.

ESTRAGON: Another day done with.

VLADIMIR: Not yet.

ESTRAGON: For me it's over and done with, no matter what happens. [*Silence.*] I heard you singing.

VLADIMIR: That's right, I remember.

ESTRAGON: That finished me. I said to myself, he's all alone, he thinks I'm gone for ever, and he sings.

VLADIMIR: One isn't master of one's moods. All day I've felt in great form. [*Pause.*] I didn't get up in the night, not once!

ESTRAGON: [*Sadly.*] You see, you piss better when I'm not there.

VLADIMIR: I missed you . . . and at the same time I was happy. Isn't that a queer thing?

ESTRAGON: [*Shocked.*] Happy?

VLADIMIR: Perhaps it's not the right word.

ESTRAGON: And now?

VLADIMIR: Now? . . . [*Joyous.*] There you are again . . . [*Indifferent.*] There we are again . . . [*Gloomy.*] There I am again.

ESTRAGON: You see, you feel worse when I'm with you. I feel better alone, too.

VLADIMIR: [*Vexed.*] Then why do you always come crawling back?

ESTRAGON: I don't know.

VLADIMIR: No, but I do. It's because you don't know how to defend yourself. I wouldn't have let them beat you.

ESTRAGON: You couldn't have stopped them.

VLADIMIR: Why not?

ESTRAGON: There were ten of them.

VLADIMIR: No, I mean before they beat you. I would

have stopped you from doing whatever it was you
were doing.

ESTRAGON: I wasn't doing anything.

VLADIMIR: Then why did they beat you?

ESTRAGON: I don't know.

VLADIMIR: Ah no, Gogo, the truth is there are things escape
you that don't escape me, you must feel it yourself.

ESTRAGON: I tell you I wasn't doing anything.

VLADIMIR: Perhaps you weren't. But it's the way of doing
it that counts, the way of doing it, if you want to go
on living.

ESTRAGON: I wasn't doing anything.

VLADIMIR: You must be happy, too, deep down, if you
only knew it.

ESTRAGON: Happy about what?

VLADIMIR: To be back with me again.

ESTRAGON: Would you say so?

VLADIMIR: Say you are, even if it's not true.

ESTRAGON: What am I to say?

VLADIMIR: Say, I am happy.

ESTRAGON: I am happy.

VLADIMIR: So am I.

ESTRAGON: So am I.

VLADIMIR: We are happy.

ESTRAGON: We are happy. [*Silence.*] What do we do now,
now that we are happy?

VLADIMIR: Wait for Godot. [ESTRAGON *groans. Silence.*]
Things have changed since yesterday.

ESTRAGON: And if he doesn't come?

VLADIMIR: [*After a moment of bewilderment.*] We'll see
when the time comes. [*Pause.*] I was saying that
things have changed here since yesterday.

ESTRAGON: Everything oozes.

VLADIMIR: Look at the tree.

ESTRAGON: It's never the same pus from one second to
the next.

VLADIMIR: The tree, look at the tree.
[ESTRAGON *looks at the tree.*]

ESTRAGON: Was it not there yesterday?

VLADIMIR: Yes, of course it was there. Do you not remember? We nearly hanged ourselves from it. But you wouldn't. Do you not remember?

ESTRAGON: You dreamt it.

VLADIMIR: Is it possible that you've forgotten already?

ESTRAGON: That's the way I am. Either I forget immediately or I never forget.

VLADIMIR: And Pozzo and Lucky, have you forgotten them too?

ESTRAGON: Pozzo and Lucky?

VLADIMIR: He's forgotten everything!

ESTRAGON: I remember a lunatic who kicked the shins off me. Then he played the fool.

VLADIMIR: That was Lucky.

ESTRAGON: I remember that. But when was it?

VLADIMIR: And his keeper, do you not remember him?

ESTRAGON: He gave me a bone.

VLADIMIR: That was Pozzo.

ESTRAGON: And all that was yesterday, you say?

VLADIMIR: Yes, of course it was yesterday.

ESTRAGON: And here where we are now?

VLADIMIR: Where else do you think? Do you not recognize the place?

ESTRAGON: [*Suddenly furious.*] Recognize! What is there to recognize? All my lousy life I've crawled about in the mud! And you talk to me about scenery! [*Looking wildly about him.*] Look at this muckheap! I've never stirred from it!

VLADIMIR: Calm yourself, calm yourself.

ESTRAGON: You and your landscapes! Tell me about the worms!

VLADIMIR: All the same, you can't tell me that this [*Gesture*] bears any resemblance to . . . [*He hesitates*]

. . . to the Macon country, for example. You can't
deny there's a big difference.

ESTRAGON: The Macon country! Who's talking to you
about the Macon country?

VLADIMIR: But you were there yourself, in the Macon
country.

ESTRAGON: No, I was never in the Macon country. I've
puked my puke of a life away here, I tell you! Here!
In the Cackon country!

VLADIMIR: But we were there together, I could swear to
it! Picking grapes for a man called . . . [*He snaps his
fingers*] . . . can't think of the name of the man, at a
place called . . . [*Snaps his fingers*] . . . can't think of
the name of the place, do you not remember?

ESTRAGON: [*A little calmer.*] It's possible. I didn't notice
anything.

VLADIMIR: But down there everything is red!

ESTRAGON: [*Exasperated.*] I didn't notice anything, I tell
you!

[*Silence.* VLADIMIR *sighs deeply.*]

VLADIMIR: You're a hard man to get on with, Gogo.

ESTRAGON: It'd be better if we parted.

VLADIMIR: You always say that, and you always come
crawling back.

ESTRAGON: The best thing would be to kill me, like the
other.

VLADIMIR: What other? [*Pause.*] What other?

ESTRAGON: Like billions of others.

VLADIMIR: [*Sententious.*] To every man his little cross.
[*He sighs.*] Till he dies. [*Afterthought.*] And is
forgotten.

ESTRAGON: In the meantime let us try and converse
calmly, since we are incapable of keeping silent.

VLADIMIR: You're right, we're inexhaustible.

ESTRAGON: It's so we won't think.

VLADIMIR: We have that excuse.

ESTRAGON: It's so we won't hear.
VLADIMIR: We have our reasons.
ESTRAGON: All the dead voices.
VLADIMIR: They make a noise like wings.
ESTRAGON: Like leaves.
VLADIMIR: Like sand.
ESTRAGON: Like leaves.
    [*Silence.*]
VLADIMIR: They all speak together.
ESTRAGON: Each one to itself.
    [*Silence.*]
VLADIMIR: Rather they whisper.
ESTRAGON: They rustle.
VLADIMIR: They murmur.
ESTRAGON: They rustle.
    [*Silence.*]
VLADIMIR: What do they say?
ESTRAGON: They talk about their lives.
VLADIMIR: To have lived is not enough for them.
ESTRAGON: They have to talk about it.
VLADIMIR: To be dead is not enough for them.
ESTRAGON: It is not sufficient.
    [*Silence.*]
VLADIMIR: They make a noise like feathers.
ESTRAGON: Like leaves.
VLADIMIR: Like ashes.
ESTRAGON: Like leaves.
    [*Long silence.*]
VLADIMIR: Say something!
ESTRAGON: I'm trying.
    [*Long silence.*]
VLADIMIR: [*In anguish.*] Say anything at all!
ESTRAGON: What do we do now?
VLADIMIR: Wait for Godot.
ESTRAGON: Ah!
    [*Silence.*]

VLADIMIR: This is awful!

ESTRAGON: Sing something.

VLADIMIR: No no! [*He reflects.*] We could start all over again perhaps.

ESTRAGON: That should be easy.

VLADIMIR: It's the start that's difficult.

ESTRAGON: You can start from anything.

VLADIMIR: Yes, but you have to decide.

ESTRAGON: True.

 [*Silence.*]

VLADIMIR: Help me!

ESTRAGON: I'm trying.

 [*Silence.*]

VLADIMIR: When you seek you hear.

ESTRAGON: You do.

VLADIMIR: That prevents you from finding.

ESTRAGON: It does.

VLADIMIR: That prevents you from thinking.

ESTRAGON: You think all the same.

VLADIMIR: No, no, impossible.

ESTRAGON: That's the idea, let's contradict each other.

VLADIMIR: Impossible.

ESTRAGON: You think so?

VLADIMIR: We're in no danger of ever thinking any more.

ESTRAGON: Then what are we complaining about?

VLADIMIR: Thinking is not the worst.

ESTRAGON: Perhaps not. But at least there's that.

VLADIMIR: That what?

ESTRAGON: That's the idea, let's ask each other questions.

VLADIMIR: What do you mean, at least there's that?

ESTRAGON: That much less misery.

VLADIMIR: True.

ESTRAGON: Well? If we gave thanks for our mercies?

VLADIMIR: What is terrible is to *have* thought.

ESTRAGON: But did that ever happen to us?

VLADIMIR: Where are all these corpses from?

59

ESTRAGON: These skeletons.
VLADIMIR: Tell me that.
ESTRAGON: True.
VLADIMIR: We must have thought a little.
ESTRAGON: At the very beginning.
VLADIMIR: A charnel-house! A charnel-house!
ESTRAGON: You don't have to look.
VLADIMIR: You can't help looking.
ESTRAGON: True.
VLADIMIR: Try as one may.
ESTRAGON: I beg your pardon?
VLADIMIR: Try as one may.
ESTRAGON: We should turn resolutely towards Nature.
VLADIMIR: We've tried that.
ESTRAGON: True.
VLADIMIR: Oh, it's not the worst, I know.
ESTRAGON: What?
VLADIMIR: To have thought.
ESTRAGON: Obviously.
VLADIMIR: But we could have done without it.
ESTRAGON: Que voulez-vous?
VLADIMIR: I beg your pardon?
ESTRAGON: Que voulez-vous?
VLADIMIR: Ah! que voulez-vous. Exactly.
[*Silence.*]
ESTRAGON: That wasn't such a bad little canter.
VLADIMIR: Yes, but now we'll have to find something else.
ESTRAGON: Let me see.
[*He takes off his hat, concentrates.*]
VLADIMIR: Let me see. [*He takes off his hat, concentrates. Long silence.*] Ah!
[*They put on their hats, relax.*]
ESTRAGON: Well?
VLADIMIR: What was I saying, we could go on from there.
ESTRAGON: What were you saying when?
VLADIMIR: At the very beginning.

ESTRAGON: The beginning of WHAT?

VLADIMIR: This evening . . . I was saying . . . I was saying . . .

ESTRAGON: I'm not a historian.

VLADIMIR: Wait . . . we embraced . . . we were happy . . . happy . . . what do we do now that we're happy . . . go on waiting . . . waiting . . . let me think . . . it's coming . . . go on waiting . . . now that we're happy . . . let me see . . . ah! The tree!

ESTRAGON: The tree?

VLADIMIR: Do you not remember?

ESTRAGON: I'm tired.

VLADIMIR: Look at it.

[*They look at the tree.*]

ESTRAGON: I see nothing.

VLADIMIR: But yesterday evening it was all black and bare. And now it's covered with leaves.

ESTRAGON: Leaves?

VLADIMIR: In a single night.

ESTRAGON: It must be the spring.

VLADIMIR: But in a single night!

ESTRAGON: I tell you we weren't here yesterday. Another of your nightmares.

VLADIMIR: And where were we yesterday evening according to you?

ESTRAGON: How do I know? In another compartment. There's no lack of void.

VLADIMIR: [*Sure of himself.*] Good. We weren't here yesterday evening. Now what did we do yesterday evening?

ESTRAGON: Do?

VLADIMIR: Try and remember.

ESTRAGON: Do . . . I suppose we blathered.

VLADIMIR: [*Controlling himself.*] About what?

ESTRAGON: Oh . . . this and that, I suppose, nothing in particular. [*With assurance.*] Yes, now I remember, yesterday evening we spent blathering about nothing in particular. That's been going on now for half a century.

VLADIMIR: You don't remember any fact, any circumstance?

ESTRAGON: [*Weary.*] Don't torment me, Didi.

VLADIMIR: The sun. The moon. Do you not remember?

ESTRAGON: They must have been there, as usual.

VLADIMIR: You didn't notice anything out of the ordinary?

ESTRAGON: Alas!

VLADIMIR: And Pozzo? And Lucky?

ESTRAGON: Pozzo?

VLADIMIR: The bones.

ESTRAGON: They were like fishbones.

VLADIMIR: It was Pozzo gave them to you.

ESTRAGON: I don't know.

VLADIMIR: And the kick.

ESTRAGON: That's right, someone gave me a kick.

VLADIMIR: It was Lucky gave it to you.

ESTRAGON: And all that was yesterday?

VLADIMIR: Show your leg.

ESTRAGON: Which?

VLADIMIR: Both. Pull up your trousers. [ESTRAGON *gives a leg to* VLADIMIR, *staggers.* VLADIMIR *takes the leg. They stagger.*] Pull up your trousers.

ESTRAGON: I can't.

[VLADIMIR *pulls up the trousers, look at the leg, lets it go.* ESTRAGON *almost falls.*]

VLADIMIR: The other. [ESTRAGON *gives the same leg.*] The other, pig! [ESTRAGON *gives the other leg. Triumphantly.*] There's the wound! Beginning to fester!

ESTRAGON: And what about it?

VLADIMIR: [*Letting go the leg.*] Where are your boots?

ESTRAGON: I must have thrown them away.

VLADIMIR: When?

ESTRAGON: I don't know.

VLADIMIR: Why?

ESTRAGON: [*Exasperated.*] I don't know why I don't know!

VLADIMIR: No, I mean why did you throw them away?

ESTRAGON: [*Exasperated.*] Because they were hurting me!

VLADIMIR: [*Triumphantly, pointing to the boots.*] There they are! [ESTRAGON *looks at the boots.*] At the very spot where you left them yesterday!
[ESTRAGON *goes towards the boots, inspects them closely.*]

ESTRAGON: They're not mine.

VLADIMIR: [*Stupefied.*] Not yours!

ESTRAGON: Mine were black. These are brown.

VLADIMIR: You're sure yours were black?

ESTRAGON: Well, they were a kind of grey.

VLADIMIR: And these are brown? Show.

ESTRAGON: [*Picking up a boot.*] Well, they're a kind of green.

VLADIMIR: Show. [ESTRAGON *hands him the boot.* VLADIMIR *inspects it, throws it down angrily.*] Well of all the –

ESTRAGON: You see, all that's a lot of bloody –

VLADIMIR: Ah! I see what it is. Yes, I see what's happened.

ESTRAGON: All that's a lot of bloody –

VLADIMIR: It's elementary. Someone came and took yours and left you his.

ESTRAGON: Why?

VLADIMIR: His were too tight for him, so he took yours.

ESTRAGON: But mine were too tight.

VLADIMIR: For you. Not for him.

ESTRAGON: [*Having tried in vain to work it out.*] I'm tired! [*Pause.*] Let's go.

VLADIMIR: We can't.

ESTRAGON: Why not?

VLADIMIR: We're waiting for Godot.

ESTRAGON: Ah! [*Pause. Despairing.*] What'll we do, what'll we do!

VLADIMIR: There's nothing we can do.

ESTRAGON: But I can't go on like this!

VLADIMIR: Would you like a radish?

ESTRAGON: Is that all there is?

VLADIMIR: There are radishes and turnips.

ESTRAGON: Are there no carrots?

VLADIMIR: No. Anyway you overdo it with your carrots.

ESTRAGON: Then give me a radish. [VLADIMIR *fumbles in his pockets, finds nothing but turnips, finally brings out a radish and hands it to* ESTRAGON, *who examines it, sniffs it.*] It's black!

VLADIMIR: It's a radish.

ESTRAGON: I only like the pink ones, you know that!

VLADIMIR: Then you don't want it?

ESTRAGON: I only like the pink ones!

VLADIMIR: Then give it back to me.

[ESTRAGON *gives it back.*]

ESTRAGON: I'll go and get a carrot.

[*He does not move.*]

VLADIMIR: This is becoming really insignificant.

ESTRAGON: Not enough.

[*Silence.*]

VLADIMIR: What about trying them?

ESTRAGON: I've tried everything.

VLADIMIR: No, I mean the boots.

ESTRAGON: Would that be a good thing?

VLADIMIR: It'd pass the time. [ESTRAGON *hesitates.*] I assure you, it'd be an occupation.

ESTRAGON: A relaxation.

VLADIMIR: A recreation.

ESTRAGON: A relaxation.

VLADIMIR: Try.

ESTRAGON: You'll help me?

VLADIMIR: I will of course.

ESTRAGON: We don't manage too badly, eh Didi, between the two of us?

VLADIMIR: Yes yes. Come on, we'll try the left first.

ESTRAGON: We always find something, eh Didi, to give us the impression we exist?

VLADIMIR: [*Impatiently.*] Yes yes, we're magicians. But let us persevere in what we have resolved, before we forget. [*He picks up a boot.*] Come on, give me your foot. [ESTRAGON *raises his foot.*] The other, hog! [ESTRAGON *raises the other foot.*] Higher! [*Wreathed together they stagger about the stage.* VLADIMIR *succeeds finally in getting on the boot.*] Try and walk. [ESTRAGON *walks.*] Well?

ESTRAGON: It fits.

VLADIMIR: [*Taking string from his pocket.*] We'll try and lace it.

ESTRAGON: [*Vehemently.*] No no, no laces, no laces!

VLADIMIR: You'll be sorry. Let's try the other. [*As before.*] Well?

ESTRAGON: [*Grudgingly.*] It fits too.

VLADIMIR: They don't hurt you?

ESTRAGON: Not yet.

VLADIMIR: Then you can keep them.

ESTRAGON: They're too big.

VLADIMIR: Perhaps you'll have socks some day.

ESTRAGON: True.

VLADIMIR: Then you'll keep them?

ESTRAGON: That's enough about these boots.

VLADIMIR: Yes, but –

ESTRAGON: [*Violently.*] Enough! [*Silence.*] I suppose I might as well sit down.
[*He looks for a place to sit down, then goes and sits down on the mound.*]

VLADIMIR: That's where you were sitting yesterday evening.

ESTRAGON: If I could only sleep.

SAMUEL BECKETT

VLADIMIR: Yesterday you slept.
ESTRAGON: I'll try.
[*He resumes his foetal posture, his head between his knees.*]
VLADIMIR: Wait. [*He goes over and sits down beside* ESTRAGON *and begins to sing in a loud voice.*]
Bye bye bye bye
Bye bye –
ESTRAGON: [*Looking up angrily.*] Not so loud!
VLADIMIR: [*Softly.*]
Bye bye bye bye
Bye bye bye bye
Bye bye bye bye
Bye bye . . .
[ESTRAGON *sleeps.* VLADIMIR *gets up softly, takes off his coat and lays it across* ESTRAGON's *shoulders, then starts walking up and down, swinging his arms to keep himself warm.* ESTRAGON *wakes with a start, jumps up, casts about wildly.* VLADIMIR *runs to him, puts his arms round him.*] There . . . there . . . Didi is there . . . don't be afraid . . .
ESTRAGON: Ah!
VLADIMIR: There . . . there . . . it's all over.
ESTRAGON: I was falling –
VLADIMIR: It's all over, it's all over.
ESTRAGON: I was on top of a –
VLADIMIR: Don't tell me! Come, we'll walk it off.
[*He takes* ESTRAGON *by the arm and walks him up and down until* ESTRAGON *refuses to go any further.*]
ESTRAGON: That's enough. I'm tired.
VLADIMIR: You'd rather be stuck there doing nothing?
ESTRAGON: Yes.
VLADIMIR: Please yourself.
[*He releases* ESTRAGON, *picks up his coat and puts it on.*]
ESTRAGON: Let's go.

VLADIMIR: We can't.

ESTRAGON: Why not?

VLADIMIR: We're waiting for Godot.

ESTRAGON: Ah! [VLADIMIR *walks up and down.*] Can you not stay still?

VLADIMIR: I'm cold.

ESTRAGON: We came too soon.

VLADIMIR: It's always at nightfall.

ESTRAGON: But night doesn't fall.

VLADIMIR: It'll fall all of a sudden, like yesterday.

ESTRAGON: Then it'll be night.

VLADIMIR: And we can go.

ESTRAGON: Then it'll be day again. [*Pause. Despairing.*] What'll we do, what'll we do!

VLADIMIR: [*Halting, violently.*] Will you stop whining! I've had about my bellyful of your lamentations!

ESTRAGON: I'm going.

VLADIMIR: [*Seeing* LUCKY's *hat.*] Well!

ESTRAGON: Farewell.

VLADIMIR: Lucky's hat. [*He goes towards it.*] I've been here an hour and never saw it. [*Very pleased.*] Fine!

ESTRAGON: You'll never see me again.

VLADIMIR: I knew it was the right place. Now our troubles are over. [*He picks up the hat, contemplates it, straightens it.*] Must have been a very fine hat. [*He puts it on in place of his own which he hands to* ESTRAGON.] Here.

ESTRAGON: What?

VLADIMIR: Hold that.

[ESTRAGON *takes Vladimir's hat.* VLADIMIR *adjusts* LUCKY's *hat on his head.* ESTRAGON *puts on* VLADIMIR's *hat in place of his own which he hands to* VLADIMIR. VLADIMIR *takes* ESTRAGON's *hat.* ESTRAGON *adjusts* VLADIMIR's *hat on his head.* VLADIMIR *puts on* ESTRAGON's *hat in place of* LUCKY's *which he hands to* ESTRAGON. ESTRAGON *takes*

67

LUCKY's *hat.* VLADIMIR *adjusts* ESTRAGON's *hat on his head.* ESTRAGON *puts on* LUCKY's *hat in place of* VLADIMIR's *which he hands to* VLADIMIR. VLADIMIR *takes his hat.* ESTRAGON *adjusts* LUCKY's *hat on his head.* VLADIMIR *puts on his hat in place of* ESTRAGON's *which he hands to* ESTRAGON. ESTRAGON *takes his hat.* VLADIMIR *adjusts his hat on his head.* ESTRAGON *puts on his hat in place of* LUCKY's *which he hands to* VLADIMIR. VLADIMIR *takes* LUCKY's *hat.* ESTRAGON *adjusts his hat on his head.* VLADIMIR *puts on* LUCKY's *hat in place of his own which he hands to* ESTRAGON. ESTRAGON *takes* VLADIMIR's *hat.* VLADIMIR *adjusts* LUCKY's *hat on his head.* ESTRAGON *hands* VLADIMIR's *hat back to* VLADIMIR *who takes it and hands it back to* ESTRAGON *who takes it and hands it back to* VLADIMIR *who takes it and throws it down.*]
How does it fit me?

ESTRAGON: How would I know?

VLADIMIR: No, but how do I look in it?
[*He turns his head coquettishly to and fro, minces like a mannequin.*]

ESTRAGON: Hideous.

VLADIMIR: Yes, but not more so than usual?

ESTRAGON: Neither more nor less.

VLADIMIR: Then I can keep it. Mine irked me. [*Pause.*] How shall I say? [*Pause.*] It itched me.
[*He takes off* LUCKY's *hat, peers into it, shakes it, knocks on the crown, puts it on again.*]

ESTRAGON: I'm going.
[*Silence.*]

VLADIMIR: Will you not play?

ESTRAGON: Play at what?

VLADIMIR: We could play at Pozzo and Lucky.

ESTRAGON: Never heard of it.

VLADIMIR: I'll do Lucky, you do Pozzo. [*He imitates*

LUCKY *sagging under the weight of his baggage.*
ESTRAGON *looks at him with stupefaction.*] Go on.

ESTRAGON: What am I to do?

VLADIMIR: Curse me!

ESTRAGON: [*After reflection.*] Naughty!

VLADIMIR: Stronger!

ESTRAGON: Gonococcus! Spirochaete!

[VLADIMIR *sways back and forth, doubled in two.*]

VLADIMIR: Tell me to think.

ESTRAGON: What?

VLADIMIR: Say, Think, pig!

ESTRAGON: Think, pig!

[*Silence.*]

VLADIMIR: I can't.

ESTRAGON: That's enough of that.

VLADIMIR: Tell me to dance.

ESTRAGON: I'm going.

VLADIMIR: Dance, hog! [*He writhes. Exit* ESTRAGON
left, precipitately.] I can't! [*He looks up, misses*
ESTRAGON.] Gogo! [*He moves wildly about the
stage. Enter* ESTRAGON *left, panting. He hastens
towards* VLADIMIR, *falls into his arms.*] There you
are again at last!

ESTRAGON: I'm accursed!

VLADIMIR: Where were you! I thought you were gone for
ever.

ESTRAGON: They're coming!

VLADIMIR: Who?

ESTRAGON: I don't know.

VLADIMIR: How many?

ESTRAGON: I don't know.

VLADIMIR: [*Triumphantly.*] It's Godot! At last! Gogo! It's
Godot! We're saved! Let's go and meet him! [*He drags*
ESTRAGON *towards the wings.* ESTRAGON *resists,
pulls himself free, exit right.*] Gogo! Come back!
[VLADIMIR *runs to extreme left, scans the horizon.*

SAMUEL BECKETT

Enter ESTRAGON *right, he hastens towards*
VLADIMIR, *falls into his arms.*] There you are again
again!

ESTRAGON: I'm in hell!

VLADIMIR: Where were you?

ESTRAGON: They're coming there too!

VLADIMIR: We're surrounded! [ESTRAGON *makes a rush
towards back.*] Imbecile! There's no way out there.
[*He takes* ESTRAGON *by the arm and drags him
towards front. Gesture towards front.*] There! Not a
soul in sight! Off you go. Quick! [*He pushes*
ESTRAGON *towards auditorium.* ESTRAGON *recoils in
horror.*] You won't? [*He contemplates auditorium.*]
Well, I can understand that. Wait till I see. [*He
reflects.*] Your only hope left is to disappear.

ESTRAGON: Where?

VLADIMIR: Behind the tree. [ESTRAGON *hesitates.*]
Quick! Behind the tree. [ESTRAGON *goes and
crouches behind the tree, realizes he is not hidden,
comes out from behind the tree.*] Decidedly this tree
will not have been of the slightest use to us.

ESTRAGON: [*Calmer.*] I lost my head. Forgive me. It
won't happen again. Tell me what to do.

VLADIMIR: There's nothing to do.

ESTRAGON: You go and stand there. [*He draws*
VLADIMIR *to extreme right and places him with his
back to the stage.*] There, don't move, and watch out.
[VLADIMIR *scans horizon, screening his eyes with his
hand.* ESTRAGON *runs and takes up same position,
extreme left. They turn their heads and look at each
other.*] Back to back like in the good old days! [*They
continue to look at each other for a moment, then
resume their watch. Long silence.*] Do you see
anything coming?

VLADIMIR: [*Turning his head.*] What?

ESTRAGON: [*Louder.*] Do you see anything coming?

70

VLADIMIR: No.
ESTRAGON: Nor I.
    [*They resume their watch. Silence.*]
VLADIMIR: You must have had a vision.
ESTRAGON: [*Turning his head.*] What?
VLADIMIR: [*Louder.*] You must have had a vision!
ESTRAGON: No need to shout!
    [*They resume their watch. Silence.*]
VLADIMIR: }
ESTRAGON: } [*Turning simultaneously.*] Do you –
VLADIMIR: Oh, pardon!
ESTRAGON: Carry on.
VLADIMIR: No no, after you.
ESTRAGON: No no, you first.
VLADIMIR: I interrupted you.
ESTRAGON: On the contrary.
    [*They glare at each other angrily.*]
VLADIMIR: Ceremonious ape!
ESTRAGON: Punctilious pig!
VLADIMIR: Finish your phrase, I tell you!
ESTRAGON: Finish your own!
    [*Silence. They draw closer, halt.*]
VLADIMIR: Moron!
ESTRAGON: That's the idea, let's abuse each other.
    [*They turn, move apart, turn again and face each other.*]
VLADIMIR: Moron!
ESTRAGON: Vermin!
VLADIMIR: Abortion!
ESTRAGON: Morpion!
VLADIMIR: Sewer-rat!
ESTRAGON: Curate!
VLADIMIR: Cretin!
ESTRAGON: [*With finality.*] Crritic!
VLADIMIR: Oh!
    [*He wilts, vanquished, and turns away.*]
ESTRAGON: Now let's make it up.

VLADIMIR: Gogo!
ESTRAGON: Didi!
VLADIMIR: Your hand!
ESTRAGON: Take it!
VLADIMIR: Come to my arms!
ESTRAGON: Your arms?
VLADIMIR: My breast!
ESTRAGON: Off we go!
    [*They embrace. They separate. Silence.*]
VLADIMIR: How time flies when one has fun!
    [*Silence.*]
ESTRAGON: What do we do now?
VLADIMIR: While waiting.
ESTRAGON: While waiting.
    [*Silence.*]
VLADIMIR: We could do our exercises.
ESTRAGON: Our movements.
VLADIMIR: Our elevations.
ESTRAGON: Our relaxations.
VLADIMIR: Our elongations.
ESTRAGON: Our relaxations.
VLADIMIR: To warm us up.
ESTRAGON: To calm us down.
VLADIMIR: Off we go.
    [VLADIMIR *hops from one foot to the other.*
    ESTRAGON *imitates him.*]
ESTRAGON: [*Stopping.*] That's enough. I'm tired.
VLADIMIR: [*Stopping.*] We're not in form. What about a
    little deep breathing?
ESTRAGON: I'm tired breathing.
VLADIMIR: You're right. [*Pause.*] Let's just do the tree,
    for the balance.
ESTRAGON: The tree?
    [VLADIMIR *does the tree, staggering about on one leg.*]
VLADIMIR: [*Stopping.*] Your turn.
    [ESTRAGON *does the tree, staggers.*]

ESTRAGON: Do you think God sees me?

VLADIMIR: You must close your eyes.

[ESTRAGON *closes his eyes, staggers worse.*]

ESTRAGON: [*Stopping, brandishing his fists, at the top of his voice.*] God have pity on me!

VLADIMIR: [*Vexed.*] And me?

ESTRAGON: On me! On me! Pity! On me!

[*Enter* POZZO *and* LUCKY. POZZO *is blind.* LUCKY *burdened as before. Rope as before, but much shorter, so that* POZZO *may follow more easily.* LUCKY *wearing a different hat. At the sight of* VLADIMIR *and* ESTRAGON *he stops short.* POZZO, *continuing on his way, bumps into him.*]

VLADIMIR: Gogo!

POZZO: [*Clutching on to* LUCKY, *who staggers.*] What is it? Who is it?

[LUCKY *falls, drops everything and brings down* POZZO *with him. They lie helpless among the scattered baggage.*]

ESTRAGON: Is it Godot?

VLADIMIR: At last! [*He goes towards the heap.*] Reinforcements at last!

POZZO: Help!

ESTRAGON: Is it Godot?

VLADIMIR: We were beginning to weaken. Now we're sure to see the evening out.

POZZO: Help!

ESTRAGON: Do you hear him?

VLADIMIR: We are no longer alone, waiting for the night, waiting for Godot, waiting for... waiting. All evening we have struggled, unassisted. Now it's over. It's already tomorrow.

POZZO: Help!

VLADIMIR: Time flows again already. The sun will set, the moon will rise, and we away... from here.

POZZO: Pity!

VLADIMIR: Poor Pozzo!

ESTRAGON: I knew it was him.

VLADIMIR: Who?

ESTRAGON: Godot.

VLADIMIR: But it's not Godot.

ESTRAGON: It's not Godot?

VLADIMIR: It's not Godot.

ESTRAGON: Then who is it?

VLADIMIR: It's Pozzo.

POZZO: Here! Here! Help me up!

VLADIMIR: He can't get up.

ESTRAGON: Let's go.

VLADIMIR: We can't.

ESTRAGON: Why not?

VLADIMIR: We're waiting for Godot.

ESTRAGON: Ah!

VLADIMIR: Perhaps he has another bone for you.

ESTRAGON: Bone?

VLADIMIR: Chicken. Do you not remember?

ESTRAGON: It was him?

VLADIMIR: Yes.

ESTRAGON: Ask him.

VLADIMIR: Perhaps we should help him first.

ESTRAGON: To do what?

VLADIMIR: To get up.

ESTRAGON: He can't get up?

VLADIMIR: He wants to get up.

ESTRAGON: Then let him get up.

VLADIMIR: He can't.

ESTRAGON: Why not?

VLADIMIR: I don't know.

[POZZO *writhes, groans, beats the ground with his fists.*]

ESTRAGON: We should ask him for the bone first. Then if he refuses we'll leave him there.

VLADIMIR: You mean we have him at our mercy?

74

ESTRAGON: Yes.

VLADIMIR: And that we should subordinate our good offices to certain conditions.

ESTRAGON: What?

VLADIMIR: That seems intelligent all right. But there's one thing I'm afraid of.

POZZO: Help!

ESTRAGON: What?

VLADIMIR: That Lucky might get going all of a sudden. Then we'd be ballocksed.

ESTRAGON: Lucky?

VLADIMIR: He's the one who went for you yesterday.

ESTRAGON: I tell you there was ten of them.

VLADIMIR: No, before that, the one that kicked you.

ESTRAGON: Is he there?

VLADIMIR: As large as life. [*Gesture towards* LUCKY.] For the moment he is inert. But he might run amuck any minute.

POZZO: Help!

ESTRAGON: And suppose we gave him a good beating, the two of us?

VLADIMIR: You mean if we fell on him in his sleep?

ESTRAGON: Yes.

VLADIMIR: That seems a good idea all right. But could we do it? Is he really asleep? [*Pause.*] No, the best would be to take advantage of Pozzo's calling for help –

POZZO: Help!

VLADIMIR: To help him –

ESTRAGON: *We* help *him*?

VLADIMIR: In anticipation of some tangible return.

ESTRAGON: And suppose he –

VLADIMIR: Let us not waste our time in idle discourse! [*Pause. Vehemently.*] Let us do something, while we have the chance! It is not every day that we are needed. Not indeed that we personally are needed.

75

Others would meet the case equally well, if not
better. To all mankind they were addressed, those
cries for help still ringing in our ears! But at this
place, at this moment of time, all mankind is us,
whether we like it or not. Let us make the most of
it, before it is too late! Let us represent worthily for
once the foul brood to which a cruel fate consigned
us! What do you say? [ESTRAGON *says nothing.*] It
is true that when with folded arms we weigh the
pros and cons we are no less a credit to our species.
The tiger bounds to the help of his congeners
without the least reflection, or else he slinks away
into the depths of the thickets. But that is not the
question. What are we doing here, *that* is the
question. And we are blessed in this, that we
happen to know the answer. Yes, in this immense
confusion one thing alone is clear. We are waiting
for Godot to come –

ESTRAGON: Ah!

POZZO: Help!

VLADIMIR: Or for night to fall. [*Pause.*] We have kept
our appointment, and that's an end to that. We are
not saints, but we have kept our appointment. How
many people can boast as much?

ESTRAGON: Billions.

VLADIMIR: You think so?

ESTRAGON: I don't know.

VLADIMIR: You may be right.

POZZO: Help!

VLADIMIR: All I know is that the hours are long, under
these conditions, and constrain us to beguile them
with proceedings which – how shall I say – which
may at first sight seem reasonable, until they become
a habit. You may say it is to prevent our reason from
foundering. No doubt. But has it not long been
straying in the night without end of the abyssal

depths? That's what I sometimes wonder. You follow
my reasoning?

ESTRAGON: [*Aphoristic for once.*] We all are born mad.
Some remain so.

POZZO: Help! I'll pay you!

ESTRAGON: How much?

POZZO: One hundred francs!

ESTRAGON: It's not enough.

VLADIMIR: I wouldn't go so far as that.

ESTRAGON: You think it's enough?

VLADIMIR: No, I mean so far as to assert that I was weak
in the head when I came into the world. But that is
not the question.

POZZO: Two hundred!

VLADIMIR: We wait. We are bored. [*He throws up his
hand.*] No, don't protest, we are bored to death,
there's no denying it. Good. A diversion comes along
and what do we do? We let it go to waste. Come, let's
get to work! [*He advances towards the heap, stops in
his stride.*] In an instant all will vanish and we'll be
alone once more, in the midst of nothingness!
[*He broods.*]

POZZO: Two hundred!

VLADIMIR: We're coming!
[*He tries to pull* POZZO *to his feet, fails, tries again,
stumbles, falls, tries to get up, fails.*]

ESTRAGON: What's the matter with you all?

VLADIMIR: Help!

ESTRAGON: I'm going.

VLADIMIR: Don't leave me! They'll kill me!

POZZO: Where am I?

VLADIMIR: Gogo!

POZZO: Help!

VLADIMIR: Help!

ESTRAGON: I'm going.

VLADIMIR: Help me up first. Then we'll go together.

ESTRAGON: You promise?

VLADIMIR: I swear it!

ESTRAGON: And we'll never come back?

VLADIMIR: Never!

ESTRAGON: We'll go to the Pyrenees.

VLADIMIR: Wherever you like.

ESTRAGON: I've always wanted to wander in the Pyrenees.

VLADIMIR: You'll wander in them.

ESTRAGON: [*Recoiling.*] Who farted?

VLADIMIR: Pozzo.

POZZO: Here! Here! Pity!

ESTRAGON: It's revolting!

VLADIMIR: Quick! Give me your hand.

ESTRAGON: I'm going. [*Pause. Louder.*] I'm going.

VLADIMIR: Well I suppose in the end I'll get up by myself.
    [*He tries, fails.*] In the fullness of time.

ESTRAGON: What's the matter with you?

VLADIMIR: Go to hell.

ESTRAGON: Are you staying there?

VLADIMIR: For the time being.

ESTRAGON: Come on, get up, you'll catch a chill.

VLADIMIR: Don't worry about me.

ESTRAGON: Come on, Didi, don't be pig-headed.
    [*He stretches out his hand which* VLADIMIR *makes
    haste to seize.*]

VLADIMIR: Pull!

    [ESTRAGON *pulls, stumbles, falls. Long silence.*]

POZZO: Help!

VLADIMIR: We've arrived.

POZZO: Who are you?

VLADIMIR: We are men.
    [*Silence.*]

ESTRAGON: Sweet mother earth!

VLADIMIR: Can you get up?

ESTRAGON: I don't know.

VLADIMIR: Try.

ESTRAGON: Not now, not now.
[*Silence.*]
POZZO: What happened?
VLADIMIR: [*Violently.*] Will you stop it, you! Pest! He
thinks of nothing but himself!
ESTRAGON: What about a little snooze?
VLADIMIR: Did you hear him? He wants to know what
happened!
ESTRAGON: Don't mind him. Sleep.
[*Silence.*]
POZZO: Pity! Pity!
ESTRAGON: [*With a start.*] What is it?
VLADIMIR: Were you asleep?
ESTRAGON: I must have been.
VLADIMIR: It's this bastard Pozzo at it again.
ESTRAGON: Make him stop it. Kick him in the crotch.
VLADIMIR: [*Striking* POZZO.] Will you stop it! Crablouse!
[POZZO *extricates himself with cries of pain and crawls
away. He stops, saws the air blindly, calling for help.*
VLADIMIR, *propped on his elbow, observes his retreat.*]
He's off! [POZZO *collapses.*] He's down!
ESTRAGON: What do we do now?
VLADIMIR: Perhaps I could crawl to him.
ESTRAGON: Don't leave me!
VLADIMIR: Or I could call to him.
ESTRAGON: Yes, call to him.
VLADIMIR: Pozzo! [*Silence.*] Pozzo! [*Silence.*] No reply.
ESTRAGON: Together.
VLADIMIR: }
ESTRAGON: } Pozzo! Pozzo!

VLADIMIR: He moved.
ESTRAGON: Are you sure his name is Pozzo?
VLADIMIR: [*Alarmed.*] Mr Pozzo! Come back! We won't
hurt you!
[*Silence.*]
ESTRAGON: We might try him with other names.

VLADIMIR: I'm afraid he's dying.

ESTRAGON: It'd be amusing.

VLADIMIR: What'd be amusing?

ESTRAGON: To try with other names, one after the other. It'd pass the time. And we'd be bound to hit on the right one sooner or later.

VLADIMIR: I tell you his name is Pozzo.

ESTRAGON: We'll soon see. [*He reflects.*] Abel! Abel!

POZZO: Help!

ESTRAGON: Got it in one!

VLADIMIR: I begin to weary of this motif.

ESTRAGON: Perhaps the other is called Cain. Cain! Cain!

POZZO: Help!

ESTRAGON: He's all humanity. [*Silence.*] Look at the little cloud.

VLADIMIR: [*Raising his eyes.*] Where?

ESTRAGON: There. In the zenith.

VLADIMIR: Well? [*Pause.*] What is there so wonderful about it?
[*Silence.*]

ESTRAGON: Let's pass on now to something else, do you mind?

VLADIMIR: I was just going to suggest it.

ESTRAGON: But to what?

VLADIMIR: Ah!
[*Silence.*]

ESTRAGON: Suppose we got up to begin with.

VLADIMIR: No harm in trying.
[*They get up.*]

ESTRAGON: Child's play.

VLADIMIR: Simple question of will-power.

ESTRAGON: And now?

POZZO: Help!

ESTRAGON: Let's go.

VLADIMIR: We can't.

ESTRAGON: Why not?

VLADIMIR: We're waiting for Godot.
ESTRAGON: Ah! [*Despairing.*] What'll we do, what'll we do!
POZZO: Help!
VLADIMIR: What about helping him?
ESTRAGON: What does he want?
VLADIMIR: He wants to get up.
ESTRAGON: Then why doesn't he?
VLADIMIR: He wants us to help him to get up.
ESTRAGON: Then why don't we? What are we waiting for?
[*They help* POZZO *to his feet, let him go. He falls.*]
VLADIMIR: We must hold him.
[*They get him up again.* POZZO *sags between them, his arms round their necks.*]
Feeling better?
POZZO: Who are you?
VLADIMIR: Do you not recognize us?
POZZO: I am blind.
[*Silence.*]
ESTRAGON: Perhaps he can see into the future.
VLADIMIR: Since when?
POZZO: I used to have wonderful sight – but are you friends?
ESTRAGON: [*Laughing noisily.*] He wants to know if we are friends!
VLADIMIR: No, he means friends of his.
ESTRAGON: Well?
VLADIMIR: We've proved we are, by helping him.
ESTRAGON: Exactly. Would we have helped him if we weren't his friends?
VLADIMIR: Possibly.
ESTRAGON: True.
VLADIMIR: Don't let's quibble about that now.
POZZO: You are not highwaymen?
ESTRAGON: Highwaymen! Do we look like highwaymen?
VLADIMIR: Damn it, can't you see the man is blind!

SAMUEL BECKETT

ESTRAGON: Damn it, so he is. [*Pause.*] So he says.
POZZO: Don't leave me!
VLADIMIR: No question of it.
ESTRAGON: For the moment.
POZZO: What time is it?
VLADIMIR: [*Inspecting the sky.*] Seven o'clock . . . eight
    o'clock . . .
ESTRAGON: That depends what time of year it is.
POZZO: Is it evening?
    [*Silence.* VLADIMIR *and* ESTRAGON *scrutinize the
    sunset.*]
ESTRAGON: It's rising.
VLADIMIR: Impossible.
ESTRAGON: Perhaps it's the dawn.
VLADIMIR: Don't be a fool. It's the west over there.
ESTRAGON: How do you know?
POZZO: [*Anguished.*] Is it evening?
VLADIMIR: Anyway it hasn't moved.
ESTRAGON: I tell you it's rising.
POZZO: Why don't you answer me?
ESTRAGON: Give us a chance.
VLADIMIR: [*Reassuring.*] It's evening, sir, it's evening,
    night is drawing nigh. My friend here would have me
    doubt it and I must confess he shook me for a
    moment. But it is not for nothing I have lived through
    this long day and I can assure you it is very near the
    end of its repertory. [*Pause.*] How do you feel now?
ESTRAGON: How much longer must we cart him round?
    [*They half release him, catch him again as he falls.*] We
    are not caryatids!
VLADIMIR: You were saying your sight used to be good,
    if I heard you right.
POZZO: Wonderful! Wonderful, wonderful sight!
    [*Silence.*]
ESTRAGON: [*Irritably.*] Expand! Expand!
VLADIMIR: Let him alone. Can't you see he's thinking of

82

the days when he was happy? [*Pause.*] *Memoria
praeteritorum bonorum* – that must be unpleasant.

ESTRAGON: We wouldn't know.

VLADIMIR: And it came on you all of a sudden?

POZZO: Quite wonderful!

VLADIMIR: I'm asking you if it came on you all of a
sudden.

POZZO: I woke up one fine day as blind as Fortune. [*Pause.*]
Sometimes I wonder if I'm not still asleep.

VLADIMIR: And when was that?

POZZO: I don't know.

VLADIMIR: But no later than yesterday –

POZZO: [*Violently.*] Don't question me! The blind have
no notion of time. The things of time are hidden from
them too.

VLADIMIR: Well just fancy that! I could have sworn it
was just the opposite.

ESTRAGON: I'm going.

POZZO: Where are we?

VLADIMIR: I couldn't tell you.

POZZO: It isn't by any chance the place known as the
Board?

VLADIMIR: Never heard of it.

POZZO: What is it like?

VLADIMIR: [*Looking around.*] It's indescribable. It's like
nothing. There's nothing. There's a tree.

POZZO: Then it's not the Board.

ESTRAGON: [*Sagging.*] Some diversion!

POZZO: Where is my menial?

VLADIMIR: He's about somewhere.

POZZO: Why doesn't he answer when I call?

ESTRAGON: I don't know. He seems to be sleeping.
Perhaps he's dead.

POZZO: What happened exactly?

ESTRAGON: Exactly!

VLADIMIR: The two of you slipped. [*Pause.*] And fell.

SAMUEL BECKETT

POZZO: Go and see is he hurt.

VLADIMIR: We can't leave you.

POZZO: You needn't both go.

VLADIMIR: [*To* ESTRAGON.] You go.

ESTRAGON: After what he did to me? Never!

POZZO: Yes yes, let your friend go, he stinks so. [*Silence.*]
    What is he waiting for?

VLADIMIR: What are you waiting for?

ESTRAGON: I'm waiting for Godot.
    [*Silence.*]

VLADIMIR: What exactly should he do?

POZZO: Well to begin with he should pull on the rope, as
    hard as he likes so long as he doesn't strangle him. He
    usually responds to that. If not he should give him a
    taste of his boot, in the face and the privates as far as
    possible.

VLADIMIR: [*To* ESTRAGON.] You see, you've nothing to
    be afraid of. It's even an opportunity to revenge
    yourself.

ESTRAGON: And if he defends himself?

POZZO: No no, he never defends himself.

VLADIMIR: I'll come flying to the rescue.

ESTRAGON: Don't take your eyes off me.
    [*He goes towards* LUCKY.]

VLADIMIR: Make sure he's alive before you start. No
    point in exerting yourself if he's dead.

ESTRAGON: [*Bending over* LUCKY.] He's breathing.

VLADIMIR: Then let him have it.
    [*With sudden fury* ESTRAGON *starts kicking* LUCKY,
    *hurling abuse at him as he does so. But he hurts his
    foot and moves away limping and groaning.* LUCKY
    stirs.]

ESTRAGON: Oh the brute!
    [*He sits down on the mound and tries to take off his
    boot. But he soon desists and disposes himself for
    sleep, his arms on his knees and his head on his arms.*]

POZZO: What's gone wrong now?

VLADIMIR: My friend has hurt himself.

POZZO: And Lucky?

VLADIMIR: So it is he?

POZZO: What?

VLADIMIR: It is Lucky?

POZZO: I don't understand.

VLADIMIR: And you are Pozzo?

POZZO: Certainly I am Pozzo.

VLADIMIR: The same as yesterday?

POZZO: Yesterday?

VLADIMIR: We met yesterday. [*Silence.*] Do you not remember?

POZZO: I don't remember having met anyone yesterday. But tomorrow I won't remember having met anyone today. So don't count on me to enlighten you.

VLADIMIR: But –

POZZO: Enough. Up pig!

VLADIMIR: You were bringing him to the fair to sell him. You spoke to us. He danced. He thought. You had your sight.

POZZO: As you please. Let me go! [VLADIMIR *moves away*.] Up!

[LUCKY *gets up, gathers up his burdens.*]

VLADIMIR: Where do you go from here?

POZZO: On.

[LUCKY, *laden down, takes his place before* POZZO.] Whip! [LUCKY *puts everything down, looks for whip, finds it, puts it into* POZZO's *hand, takes up everything again.*] Rope!

[LUCKY *puts everything down, puts end of the rope into* POZZO's *hand, takes up everything again.*]

VLADIMIR: What is there in the bag?

POZZO: Sand. [*He jerks the rope.*] On!

VLADIMIR: Don't go yet!

POZZO: I'm going.

VLADIMIR: What do you do when you fall far from help!

POZZO: We wait till we can get up. Then we go on. On!

VLADIMIR: Before you go tell him to sing!

POZZO: Who?

VLADIMIR: Lucky.

POZZO: To sing?

VLADIMIR: Yes. Or to think. Or to recite.

POZZO: But he's dumb.

VLADIMIR: Dumb!

POZZO: Dumb. He can't even groan.

VLADIMIR: Dumb! Since when?

POZZO: [*Suddenly furious.*] Have you not done tormenting me with your accursed time! It's abominable! When! When! One day, is that not enough for you, one day like any other day, one day he went dumb, one day I went blind, one day we'll go deaf, one day we were born, one day we shall die, the same day, the same second, is that not enough for you? [*Calmer.*] They give birth astride of a grave, the light gleams an instant, then it's night once more. [*He jerks the rope.*] On!

[*Exeunt* POZZO *and* LUCKY. VLADIMIR *follows them to the edge of the stage, looks after them. The noise of falling, reinforced by mimic of* VLADIMIR, *announces that they are down again. Silence.* VLADIMIR *goes towards* ESTRAGON, *contemplates him a moment, then shakes him awake.*]

ESTRAGON: [*Wild gestures, incoherent words. Finally.*] Why will you never let me sleep?

VLADIMIR: I felt lonely.

ESTRAGON: I was dreaming I was happy.

VLADIMIR: That passed the time.

ESTRAGON: I was dreaming that –

VLADIMIR: [*Violently.*] Don't tell me! [*Silence.*] I wonder is he really blind.

ESTRAGON: Blind? Who?

VLADIMIR: Pozzo.

ESTRAGON: Blind?

VLADIMIR: He told us he was blind.

ESTRAGON: Well what about it?

VLADIMIR: It seemed to me he saw us.

ESTRAGON: You dreamt it. [*Pause.*] Let's go. We can't. Ah! [*Pause.*] Are you sure it wasn't him?

VLADIMIR: Who?

ESTRAGON: Godot.

VLADIMIR: But who?

ESTRAGON: Pozzo.

VLADIMIR: Not at all! [*Less sure.*] Not at all! [*Still less sure.*] Not at all!

ESTRAGON: I suppose I might as well get up. [*He gets up painfully.*] Ow! Didi!

VLADIMIR: I don't know what to think any more.

ESTRAGON: My feet! [*He sits down, tries to take off his boots.*] Help me!

VLADIMIR: Was I sleeping, while the others suffered? Am I sleeping now? Tomorrow, when I wake, or think I do, what shall I say of today? That with Estragon my friend, at this place, until the fall of night, I waited for Godot? That Pozzo passed, with his carrier, and that he spoke to us? Probably. But in all that what truth will there be? [ESTRAGON, *having struggled with his boots in vain, is dozing off again.* VLADIMIR *stares at him.*] He'll know nothing. He'll tell me about the blows he received and I'll give him a carrot. [*Pause.*] Astride of a grave and a difficult birth. Down in the hole, lingeringly, the grave-digger puts on the forceps. We have time to grow old. The air is full of our cries. [*He listens.*] But habit is a great deadener. [*He looks again at* ESTRAGON.] At me too someone is looking, of me too someone is saying, he is sleeping, he knows nothing, let him sleep on. [*Pause.*] I can't go on! [*Pause.*] What have I said?

[*He goes feverishly to and fro, halts finally at extreme left, broods. Enter* BOY *right. He halts. Silence.*]

BOY: Mister . . . [VLADIMIR *turns.*] Mr Albert . . .

VLADIMIR: Off we go again. [*Pause.*] Do you not recognize me?

BOY: No, sir.

VLADIMIR: It wasn't you came yesterday.

BOY: No, sir.

VLADIMIR: This is your first time.

BOY: Yes, sir.

    [*Silence.*]

VLADIMIR: You have a message from Mr Godot.

BOY: Yes, sir.

VLADIMIR: He won't come this evening.

BOY: No, sir.

VLADIMIR: But he'll come tomorrow.

BOY: Yes, sir.

VLADIMIR: Without fail.

BOY: Yes, sir.

    [*Silence.*]

VLADIMIR: Did you meet anyone?

BOY: No, sir.

VLADIMIR: Two other . . . [*He hesitates*] . . . men?

BOY: I didn't see anyone, sir.

    [*Silence.*]

VLADIMIR: What does he do, Mr Godot? [*Silence.*] Do you hear me?

BOY: Yes, sir.

VLADIMIR: Well?

BOY: He does nothing, sir.

    [*Silence.*]

VLADIMIR: How is your brother?

BOY: He's sick, sir.

VLADIMIR: Perhaps it was he came yesterday.

BOY: I don't know, sir.

    [*Silence.*]

VLADIMIR: [*Softly.*] Has he a beard, Mr Godot?
BOY: Yes, sir.
VLADIMIR: Fair or . . . [*He hesitates*] . . . or black?
BOY: I think it's white, sir.
    [*Silence.*]
VLADIMIR: Christ have mercy on us!
    [*Silence.*]
BOY: What am I to tell Mr Godot, sir?
VLADIMIR: Tell him . . . [*He hesitates*] . . . tell him you saw
    me and that . . . [*He hesitates*] . . . that you saw me.
    [*Pause.* VLADIMIR *advances, the* BOY *recoils.*
    VLADIMIR *halts, the* BOY *halts. With sudden*
    violence.] You're sure you saw me, you won't come
    and tell me tomorrow that you never saw me!
    [*Silence.* VLADIMIR *makes a sudden spring forward,*
    the BOY *avoids him and exit running. Silence. The*
    sun sets, the moon rises. As in Act One. VLADIMIR
    stands motionless and bowed. ESTRAGON *wakes,*
    takes off his boots, gets up with one in each hand and
    goes and puts them down centre front, then goes
    towards VLADIMIR.]
ESTRAGON: What's wrong with you?
VLADIMIR: Nothing.
ESTRAGON: I'm going.
VLADIMIR: So am I.
ESTRAGON: Was I long asleep?
VLADIMIR: I don't know.
    [*Silence.*]
ESTRAGON: Where shall we go?
VLADIMIR: Not far.
ESTRAGON: Oh yes, let's go far away from here.
VLADIMIR: We can't.
ESTRAGON: Why not?
VLADIMIR: We have to come back tomorrow.
ESTRAGON: What for?
VLADIMIR: To wait for Godot.

ESTRAGON: Ah! [*Silence.*] He didn't come?

VLADIMIR: No.

ESTRAGON: And now it's too late.

VLADIMIR: Yes, now it's night.

ESTRAGON: And if we dropped him? [*Pause.*] If we dropped him?

VLADIMIR: He'd punish us. [*Silence. He looks at the tree.*] Everything's dead but the tree.

ESTRAGON: [*Looking at the tree.*] What is it?

VLADIMIR: It's the tree.

ESTRAGON: Yes, but what kind?

VLADIMIR: I don't know. A willow.

[ESTRAGON *draws* VLADIMIR *towards the tree. They stand motionless before it. Silence.*]

ESTRAGON: Why don't we hang ourselves?

VLADIMIR: With what?

ESTRAGON: You haven't got a bit of rope?

VLADIMIR: No.

ESTRAGON: Then we can't.

[*Silence.*]

VLADIMIR: Let's go.

ESTRAGON: Wait, there's my belt.

VLADIMIR: It's too short.

ESTRAGON: You could hang on to my legs.

VLADIMIR: And who'd hang on to mine?

ESTRAGON: True.

VLADIMIR: Show all the same. [ESTRAGON *loosens the cord that holds up his trousers which, much too big for him, fall about his ankles. They look at the cord.*] It might do at a pinch. But is it strong enough?

ESTRAGON: We'll soon see. Here.

[*They each take an end of the cord and pull. It breaks. They almost fall.*]

VLADIMIR: Not worth a curse.

[*Silence.*]

ESTRAGON: You say we have to come back tomorrow?

VLADIMIR: Yes.

ESTRAGON: Then we can bring a good bit of rope.

VLADIMIR: Yes.

[*Silence.*]

ESTRAGON: Didi.

VLADIMIR: Yes.

ESTRAGON: I can't go on like this.

VLADIMIR: That's what you think.

ESTRAGON: If we parted? That might be better for us.

VLADIMIR: We'll hang ourselves tomorrow. [*Pause.*] Unless Godot comes.

ESTRAGON: And if he comes?

VLADIMIR: We'll be saved.

[VLADIMIR *takes off his hat* [*Lucky's*], *peers inside it, feels about inside it, shakes it, knocks on the crown, puts it on again.*]

ESTRAGON: Well? Shall we go?

VLADIMIR: Pull on your trousers.

ESTRAGON: What?

VLADIMIR: Pull on your trousers.

ESTRAGON: You want me to pull off my trousers?

VLADIMIR: Pull ON your trousers.

ESTRAGON: [*Realizing his trousers are down.*] True. [*He pulls up his trousers.*]

VLADIMIR: Well? Shall we go?

ESTRAGON: Yes, let's go.

[*They do not move.*]

CURTAIN